# Don't Ask

# HILARY FREEMAN

PICCADILLY PRESS • LONDON

First published in Great Britain in 2009
by Piccadilly Press Ltd,
5 Castle Road, London NW1 8PR
www.piccadillypress.co.uk

A catalogue record for this book is available
from the British Library

ISBN: 978 1 85340 997 4 (paperback)

1 3 5 7 9 10 8 6 4 2

Printed in the UK by CPI Bookmarque, Croydon, CR0 4TD
Cover design by Patrick Knowles

**Mixed Sources**
Product group from well-managed
forests and other controlled sources
www.fsc.org Cert no. TT-COC-002227
© 1996 Forest Stewardship Council
FSC

*This book is dedicated to my grandma,*
*Thilde 'Safta' Brook,*
*in celebration of her 90th birthday,*
*and to the memory of my late grandpa,*
*Sid 'Saba' Brook.*

# Chapter 1

♡

*Jack was perfect. And that was the problem.*

*I knew I should have been congratulating myself on being the luckiest girl in the world, on winning the boyfriend lottery, but instead I couldn't help wondering: if Jack was perfect, then what was wrong with him?*

*You see, I know very well that nobody is perfect, least of all me. A perfect girlfriend wouldn't have done what I've done. A perfect girlfriend wouldn't even have thought of it. Miss Perfect would have been content to live happily ever after with her lovely, handsome, funny, clever, ideal boyfriend, without giving his impeccable wonderfulness a second thought. Indeed, she wouldn't have possessed a cynical bone in her body or a suspicious notion in her perfectly oval little head. But I'm not her, I'm me (which I'm kind of glad about, as she sounds rather dull). I'm the girl who always has to pick the scab off her knee, just as it's starting to heal nicely. I'm the girl who'll take her mobile phone apart to see how it works on the inside, and then be unable to put it back together again.*

*I'll make no excuses for what I've done, except to state: I simply couldn't help myself.*


It all started as a game, a challenge, which grew out of a notion.

'How are things going with Jack?' asked Katie, one rainy Saturday afternoon three months ago, as we were lounging around in my bedroom, variously surfing the net, painting each other's toenails and discussing our half-term plans (even though we'd only just gone back to school after the Christmas holidays).

'Good,' I said. 'He's great. But there are a few things that have been bothering me . . .'

The first bit is not actually true. Katie didn't ask me about Jack. I brought up the subject myself because I was dying for her to ask and she just kept ignoring my hints. In her defence, my boyfriend had become my favourite – some would say virtually my only – topic of conversation over the previous few months and, patient as Katie is, she was beginning to tire of my endless musings on his character (not to mention his looks, tastes, clothes, interests and ambitions). Fair enough, I suppose. But personally, I think she was failing in her duties as my best friend. Commandment number one: thou shalt listen without complaint, protest or interruption. Which, I noted, I would be sure to remind her of next time she bored me rigid moaning about her mum's new boyfriend.

What really happened was this.

One Saturday afternoon. In my bedroom, etc, etc . . .

'Katie,' I asked, in my best pleading voice, a few minutes after we'd last put the subject to rest. 'Can I ask you something about Jack?'

'Uh-huh,' she muttered, without looking up. I'm sure that if her eyelids hadn't been in the way I would have seen her eyeballs rolling back in her head. 'What is it now?'

'Well,' I said, more brightly now that I had her reluctant attention. 'There are a few things that have been bothering me. You know we were talking about how he won't talk about his ex? I've been trying really hard not to let it bug me, but I still don't understand why he won't.'

She sighed, audibly.

'No, but really, Katie,' I tried again, 'I know she finished with him, and so he was probably upset and all, but it was over a year ago and he still goes all funny every time anything to do with the past comes up. I just want to know what went wrong, because I don't have a clue what happened. Why did she break up with him?'

'I don't get why you need to know,' said Katie, in a kindly but exasperated tone. 'You're happy with him, he treats you brilliantly and you fancy him loads, so why does it matter why his ex dumped him? If she hadn't done it, then you'd never have met him, would you?'

'True,' I said, and I pondered her point for a moment. 'But he's so lovely and amazing to be with, why would anybody *not* want to be with him? I know *I* could never dream of dumping him. And why won't he talk about it? Or her? At all? Ever?'

'Not *everybody* likes talking about their relationships *ad infinitum*,' Katie replied, raising her left eyebrow. 'Some people think it's a turnoff to bleat on about their exes. And just because he's perfect for you, doesn't mean he was perfect for Anne or Amanda, or whatever her name was.'

I knew she had deliberately chosen the wrong names, just to be annoying. 'Alex,' I corrected. 'Her name was Alex. Alex Porter. That's about all I do know about her. That and the fact she was a huge football fan, like Jack.'

'Alex, Schmalex. Stop worrying about her. I'm sure she hasn't given you a second thought.' Katie started fiddling around on my computer keyboard. 'Come on, why don't we see if we've got any new friend requests on Topfriendz?'

'In a minute,' I told her, ignoring her attempt at a distraction. 'But it's not just Alex,' I continued. 'It's other things too. I mean, I hardly know anything about when Jack was younger. I know his dad died when he was twelve, but that's it. Don't you think that's weird?'

Katie took a deep breath and gave me a patronising little smile. 'No, not really.' She paused. 'Lily, hon, I mean this in the nicest possible way, but can you just shut up about it and simply enjoy being with Jack, OK?'

'OK,' I agreed, because there's no point continuing a conversation with someone who doesn't want to take part. But I had no intention of letting the subject drop for long.

As Katie knew very well, I'm not the sort of person who can 'just shut up and enjoy' being with a guy. According to my mother, I'm indomitable – she probably chose the word because she knew I'd have to look it up – which is a polite way of saying a pain in the backside, who always does what she wants. I discovered that there's another word, rambunctious, which means almost the same thing. As a description, I like it better because it makes me picture an out-of-control sheep bumping around in a small room, knocking things over. That just about sums up my life. And my relationships.

For most people, dating someone new is a bit like playing pass the parcel – although, usually, without the cheesy music. On your first date, your boyfriend is a neat package, wrapped in shiny paper; he's made an effort, bought some new aftershave, he's careful what he says and he minds his manners. Gradually, as time passes and you spend more time together, the sheets of shiny wrapping paper fall away and you start to uncover his true personality. Some of the layers reveal good surprises (he's generous, he enjoys the same films), others disappointing ones (he never changes his socks, he likes Westlife), and so little by little, you discover his traits and his flaws, his talents and his phobias. If you're lucky – and keep on playing until the very end – you'll tear

5

off the last sheet to find you've won the prize of a great relationship, with someone you know inside out. I know this analogy doesn't entirely work, as the package in pass the parcel gets smaller and smaller – which means you'd end up going out with Tom Thumb (or Tom Cruise) – but I'm afraid it's the best I can come up with right now.

Anyway, owing to my out-of-control-sheep-like tendencies, the pass the parcel approach to dating doesn't do anything for me. Call me greedy, but I need to know everything and I need to know it NOW. I don't like mystery or suspense, and patience is one of the many virtues I don't possess. Give me a book and I'll – inadvisably – turn straight to the last page to find out what happens at the end. Invariably, what I read there won't make much sense, and it will spoil the two hundred or so pages that go before, but knowing this won't stop me repeating my mistake. I don't understand how anybody can wait a whole week until the next episode of their favourite drama. I have to go online and look on a website to find out what happens next. Then I'll eagerly read my way through the episode synopses for the whole series and, after that, I'll Google the spoilers for the next series, the one that hasn't even finished filming yet. My dad always says: 'Show Lily a cliff-hanger and she'll find a way to abseil down it.' He thinks he's hilarious.

It's not just because I'm impatient that Jack's refusal to talk about his past bothered me so much. Mainly, it just didn't make any sense. He was so open and frank about everything else, even things that other people don't like talking about (such as puking and walking in on your mum when you shouldn't). But whenever I mentioned his last girlfriend or his childhood, his eyes would glaze over and I'd feel like I was being sucked into two vast black holes. As far as the files marked *Dad* and *Alex* were concerned, anyone would think he'd signed the Official Secrets Act.

Katie knew all this (mainly because I told her a hundred times). She said she was sure there was nothing to find out. But if there was, she said, it could only be bad news, so I shouldn't go there. Her imagined 'explanations' were not very helpful. 'Maybe his dad was a serial killer and is actually in prison,' she once suggested. 'Or maybe he found out his dad had an affair with Alex's mum years ago and that they're really brother and sister.'

She didn't suggest either of these that Saturday because, clearly, she didn't want to talk about Jack at all that afternoon. All she did want to do was to mess around on Topfriendz.com, the new networking site that we'd both signed up to about a month before. She preferred logging on at my house because she and her brother share a computer, and she couldn't be sure he wouldn't hack into her account. Katie took Topfriendz very seriously – she already had about three hundred friends. I only had sixty-five because I had a boyfriend. And a life. And a password that was impossible to remember.

I've never really got the point of networking sites.

Online friendships are rubbish. From what I can tell, you have two types of friends: the ones you like, see and speak to in real life, and the ones you don't. As far as the latter are concerned, there's usually a good reason. Since I'd joined Topfriendz, I'd been stalked by a girl from primary school who kept asking me join her Rangers group (as if), and I'd accidentally invited all my 'friends' to go shoe shopping with me on the same afternoon, by pressing the wrong button. The girl from primary school was delighted. She probably thought we could buy some nice, sensible, ranging shoes together. I have absolutely no idea what ranging shoes are but I imagine them to be green, with chunky soles and thick laces. I wouldn't be surprised if primary school girl isn't still standing outside Clarks, wondering where I've got to.

Katie had twelve new friend requests when we logged on, and I had just one. His name was Igor and he said he *liked very much my picture and wanted to make talk* with me. He was twenty-three and had a moustache. Katie said she'd show me how to set my profile to private.

While Katie dealt with her requests, I started thinking about Jack again. He didn't have a Topfriendz profile because he thought it was a waste of time and, unlike me, wasn't so worried about missing out that he couldn't stick to his principles. And then I thought, I wonder if Alex is on Topfriendz? If she is, I'll be able to see what she looks like, and what she likes doing, and even who her friends are. I couldn't believe I hadn't come up with this idea before.

'Katie,' I said excitedly. 'Give me a go.'

'I thought you weren't bothered,' she said, mimicking my own words. 'That online friendships were rubbish.'

'Mostly, they are. But I've had a genius idea. Shove up.' I squeezed on to the chair beside her and gently pushed her hands away from the keyboard. After a bit of fiddling, I found the search box and started typing in Alex's name. I'd got as far as the 'e' when Katie groaned.

'Lily, I can't believe you're looking her up!' But her voice was no longer disapproving, or bored. She sounded quite excited.

'I know I shouldn't . . . but I can't resist,' I said. We giggled together. 'I wonder if she's under Alex or Alexandra?'

She was under Alex. There were several other Alex Porters, but the others all lived in America. Or were men.

'Is that her?' cried Katie. 'Alex Porter, age seventeen, St Edmund's Sixth Form College?'

'Yes, I think so.' My heart was beating faster. There, in front of me, was a picture of the girl whom my boyfriend had loved for two years, and who had seemingly broken his heart so badly that he couldn't even mention her name without clamming up. She was pretty in an unthreatening way and she had a warm smile. 'She looks . . . normal,' I said. 'I mean, she looks just like an ordinary girl. Like us, only a bit older. Nice. Friendly.'

'What did you expect? A monster?'

'I don't know. Maybe I thought she'd look like a supermodel. Or be really cold and snooty-looking. Or have a head that spun around.'

'So do you feel better, having seen her?' asked Katie, who clearly thought that was the end of the matter.

'Yes,' I said. I hesitated. 'And no. I just wish I could see her whole profile. And talk to her.' Somewhere, deep inside my cluttered and very disorganised mind, the germ of an idea was beginning to grow: a way of satisfying my curiosity about Jack and setting my mind to rest, once and for all. The internet is supposed to be a way of sourcing information, isn't it?

'Sorry, Lil. The only way you can do that is if you . . .' Katie must have noticed the mischievous glint in my eye. 'No, Lily, you can't!'

'Why not?' I said. 'She's two years older than us, she lives on the other side of the city, she doesn't know any of our friends, she went to a different school in a different area, and, most importantly, Jack isn't on Topfriendz. So who would ever know?'

'It's too risky,' said Katie, grinning despite herself. 'Anyway, she'd never accept you as a friend if she knew who you were.'

'But she won't.' I started thinking aloud. 'And I can change my profile. I can use a different email address and have a new name. I can even be someone else entirely if I want to be.' I felt breathless, naughty, like a little girl about to do something her parents have told her never to do.

'Won't she think it's a bit weird if some girl she's never heard of pitches up and starts asking questions about her ex-boyfriend?'

'You don't have much faith in me, do you, Kay? I won't ask straight away, obviously. I'll get to know her first. And when I've got my answers I'll just delete my profile and disappear. Nobody will ever know.'

'Don't do it,' said Katie. She looked suddenly serious. 'You'll regret it, I know you will.'

'Maybe,' I said, without conviction. 'But if you don't ask you don't get.' I'd already made my decision, and Katie knew it. 'At least I'll stop going on about Alex all the time. It's the perfect way to find out what happened with Jack. She might even know about his dad.'

'True. But please be careful, Lily.'

'Course I will,' I said. 'But what could possibly go wrong?'

# Chapter 2

♡

If people ask, I always tell them that Jack and I met at a party. But if I'm going to be precise, we actually met *outside* a party, on a damp stone wall in the back garden of 29 Elmsmere Road.

The party itself – Sophy Richards' sixteenth – was a big yawn, full of virtually the same people as at every other party I ever go to. It was as if somebody had used one of those sci-fi transporter machines to beam my whole year into Sophy's living room, adding a few random extras and replacing the teachers with parents who skulked about upstairs, occasionally appearing to ask for the music to be turned down. Everyone was talking to the same people they always talk to, dancing to the same tracks, with the same stupid expressions on their faces. It even smelled the same, like eau de B.O. mixed with sickly-sweet alcopop fumes and stale cheese and onion crisps.

I was especially disappointed because I'd been looking forward to it all week, planning my outfit with Katie and anticipating all kinds of exciting possibilities, all of which involved people I hadn't yet met. That was, of course, where I went wrong; in my experience, you only enjoy the events you have to be dragged along to. It's like an equation in maths: anticipation multiplied by expectation is in inverse proportion to actual enjoyment, or something like that (clearly I can't do equations). Maybe if they taught maths using real life examples, instead of 'x's and 'y's, it would make more sense.

By ten o'clock I'd had enough. Katie was too busy examining the tonsils of a boy in the year above to notice, but even if I could have dragged her away we couldn't leave. Dad wasn't due to pick us up for two hours and we didn't have enough money for a cab. So I decided to take myself outside for a change of scene and to kill some time. It was an unexpectedly warm October evening, the last gasp of summer before it croaked for good. I circled the garden twice, pretending not to notice the snogging couples and then sat myself down on a stone wall, hoping something interesting might happen. The wall was hard and uneven and slightly wet from an earlier rain shower, and I couldn't get comfortable. I folded my skirt over, to cushion my bum, then shuffled around and swung my legs back and forth in time to the pounding bass line that was bleeding from the house. Feeling sleepy, I rested my elbows in my lap and cradled my chin with the backs of my hands. My eyelids began to flicker shut . . .

'Are you all right?'

'What?' I sat bolt upright and swung my legs over the wall, twisting my body around to face the owner of the voice. I peered through startled eyes. It was a boy, tall and stocky, with thick, sandy hair. 'Yes, I'm fine.'

'Oh, I'm sorry. I thought you were crying,' he said. He sounded concerned and embarrassed and that made me warm to him instantly.

'No, no. I was just . . . never mind.'

'Now I feel like an idiot,' said the guy.

'Don't. It's nice of you to bother. Most people wouldn't. My grandma fell over on the high street once and loads of people walked straight past her. Some of them even stepped over her.'

'That's awful,' he said. 'I wouldn't step over your grandma.'

'I'm glad to hear it. Except she's actually dead and buried now, so technically, it would be OK.'

'Oh,' he mumbled. 'Sorry . . . again.'

'No need to be,' I said, aware that this was probably the most awkward opening to a conversation I'd ever experienced. I changed the subject. 'I didn't see you inside the party.'

'That's because I've only just arrived.' He smiled. 'OK if I sit down?'

I nodded.

'I wasn't invited – I'm just here to pick up my sister. I'm a bit early, so she'll kill me if I drag her out now. Ruth Parmiter, do you know her?'

'No, sorry, I don't,' I said, observing him as he sat himself down next to me, close enough so that I could feel the warmth from his body, but not too close. He frowned as he noticed the dampness of the wall seeping through his jeans, but he didn't comment on it.

'So what's your name?' he asked, raising his eyebrows expectantly.

I could just have told him, but now I'd woken up I was in a mischievous mood, full of energy that I hadn't been able to expend at the party. I chewed my lip. 'Guess.'

He looked me up and down, and then back again, his eyes big and bright. 'Jessica?' he suggested.

'Not even close,' I said, with a smirk.

'Really? You know you *do* look like a Jessica.'

'And what does a Jessica look like?'

'Ooh, pretty, dark, a bit mysterious, I don't know. I guess I'm thinking of all the Jessicas I've known before – the ones in my class at school. There were three of them.'

'And they were all pretty, dark and mysterious?'

'No.' He smiled, cheekily. 'Actually, one of them was ginger.' He paused, checking himself. 'Not that I have anything against gingers. I was trying to be flattering.'

I felt a warm glow spread across my cheeks. So he

liked me? I caught his eye and then quickly looked away again. I once read in a magazine that this is what girls do when they like someone – look deep into a boy's eyes for a second, and then lower their eyes, bashfully. *Body Language for Beginners*, the article was called. After reading it, Katie and I spent days practising some of the 'moves' at school. None of them seemed to work for us, but that could have been because we accompanied them with raucous, wet-yourself-level giggling. Or because the boys at our school don't read articles entitled *Body Language for Beginners*, and so remain clueless about the hidden meaning of a hair flick or a lip lick.

I digress. The point is, my inability to make eye contact with him for more than a second wasn't intentional. I just couldn't do it. Looking directly in his eyes was almost as uncomfortable as staring straight into the sun. I needed sunglasses, or one of those pieces of cardboard with a hole in you use to see an eclipse. A boy filter.

'Come on, try again,' I said, after an awkward silence that seemed to last as long as a double maths lesson, but was really only about ten seconds.

'OK.' He sighed. 'What about, um, Britney?'

'As if!'

'Sorry. Christina?'

'Now you're just being silly,' I said. 'You've got to try properly.'

'Then you've got to give me a clue.'

'No, that's too easy,' I said. 'I want to make you work.'

'Fine. Then I'll start at A. Stop me if I get it right. Let me see . . . Abigail. Agatha. Ada. Adele. Amanda. Anna. Aisha. Alicia. Alison. Amy. Anastasia . . .' He spoke each name slowly, pronouncing every syllable separately, as if he was daring me to stop him at any moment. In between names, he grinned at me, his eyes twinkling with mirth.

If he thought he could bore me into submission, he had another think coming. I've got a very high boredom threshold; I even sat through the whole of *The Lord of the Rings* without complaining, because Dad bet me I couldn't. I looked at him, impassive, and folded my arms across each other, holding them at my waist. 'I'm waiting,' I said, when he got to Bettina and stopped. 'I haven't got all night.'

'Er, Beezlebub . . .'

'That's not a name!'

'Yes it is,' he said. 'It's the devil's name. I read it somewhere.'

'It's not a girl's name, then. The devil is a guy.'

'Mmm, I'm starting to wonder about that . . .'

'Ha ha. OK, I'll give you a clue. Someone famous has got my name. Although, obviously, I had it first. And mine is better!'

He scratched the crown of his head, comically. 'Nicole?'

I rolled my eyes.

'Scarlet?'

'No. Think British. Think music.'

'Amy? No, I already said that one. Cheryl? Nicola? Sarah? Kimberley?'

'No, no, no and no. Oh, and no to Nadine too. Think flower.'

'Rose. Um, Daisy. Um . . .' A look of recognition crossed his face. 'Not Lily?'

'Yes!' I shouted. 'I thought you were never going to get there.'

'You should have more faith,' he said, laughing. 'Hello Lily. My name's Jack. Jack Parmiter.'

After that, we sat and chatted for over an hour, until the outlines of the stones in the wall had imprinted themselves on the backs of my thighs. I learned that Jack was seventeen, had recently moved to my area with his mum and younger sister, and had just passed his driving test at the first attempt. He was in the Sixth Form at the big college in the next borough, loved football, practised some kind of martial art (I instantly forgot which one – they're all the same to me), and wanted to be a graphic designer. Best of all, he was single and, it turned out, strangely rather partial to me. When I said I was getting cold, Jack took off his jacket and draped it over my shoulders, gently moving my hair out of the way and accidentally on purpose brushing my face with his fingertips. I could tell he was preparing to kiss me, and my heart began to thump against my chest wall in anticipation. I was thinking about whether I should lean in towards him, when we were interrupted by a girl who appeared to have come outside looking for him.

'Where have you been?' she said indignantly, ignoring me altogether. I recognised her from the year below me at school. Like Jack, she was fair and big-boned; she looked much older than fourteen. 'Sophy told me you were out here.'

'Hello Ruth,' said Jack. 'This is Lily. Lily, this is my sister, Ruth.'

I smiled and nodded. My heart was still beating fast, in expectation of a kiss that hadn't happened.

Ruth looked me up and down, clocked the fact I was wearing Jack's jacket and gave me a disdainful glance. She said simply, 'All right,' and then she turned back to Jack. 'How come you're out here? I thought you hadn't turned up.'

Jack smiled at her. 'I thought you'd be pleased not to have to come home early,' he said. The tone of his voice was different; he sounded older, protective, kind of like a dad.

'Yeah, but you could have told me that you were,' she shook her head in my direction, ' . . . you know, out here.'

'Sorry, I lost track of time.' He looked at me, apologetically, and stood up, smoothing down the back of his jeans with his hand. 'Give me a minute, Ruth. Why don't you go and get your coat.'

'Oh, right.' She smirked at us, turned, and walked back towards the house, looking behind her for a second just before she went in through the patio doors.

Jack held out his hand to me, helping me up from the wall. I could feel my dress sticking to my tights, the material all creased up and slightly soggy. 'Keep the jacket if you want,' he said. 'You can give it back to me another time.'

'It's OK, my dad will be here in a second and I've got a jacket inside,' I said. I let him lift it from my shoulders, hoping that the kiss might at last materialise, but the moment had gone. Instead, he leaned to the left and gave me a peck on the cheek.

'Can I have your number, Lily?'

'Sure,' I said, trying not to sound disappointed. He typed it straight into his phone, gave me another peck and promised to call. Then, with a smile, he headed inside.

I told Katie all about Jack in whispers, as we huddled together conspiratorially in the back of Dad's car.

'So that's where you got to,' she said. 'God Lily, only you could go to a party and pick up someone's lift home!'

'It's my special talent. Anyway, he's only seventeen. Not even a whole two years older than us.'

I glanced at Dad in the mirror. He was pretending to be concentrating hard on the road, but I knew he was straining to hear what I'd been up to. He hates it when I sit in the back with a friend. 'I'm not a free taxi service, you know,' he always says.

'Yes, but he's got a car,' Katie said, a little too loudly. I saw Dad's shoulders rise a fraction.

'Shh,' I said. We both giggled. 'You're just jealous.'

Katie leaned in closer, so that her mouth was right by my ear. It tickled. 'Did you snog him?'

'No, but he said he's going to call me.'

She squeezed my arm. 'Excellent,' she said. And then in a loud, bright voice, the cheeky cow announced, 'Lily's got a new boyfriend, Mr Lawton, and he drives a Vauxhall Astra,' and Dad almost swerved into the pavement.

# Chapter 3

♡

*I don't feel guilty about what I did. Not really. What someone doesn't know can't hurt them, right? And it isn't as if I murdered anyone. Nobody died; in fact, you could argue that the opposite is true. I didn't steal or beat or disrespect anyone. I didn't happy-slap. I didn't betray or cheat or swindle, or kiss and tell. I didn't even gossip or swear or spit. No one was left bleeding or bruised, nobody lost anything at all. I just told the teeniest lie, a little white lie, a lie as light as a feather.*

*People always says it's good to be creative, to use your imagination. That's all I did: I invented a new persona. I changed my name, my identity, my profile – I pretended to be someone I'm not. But how can that be any more terrible than being me? Names are just labels; hobbies and interests just a collection of activities you pick up along the way and deposit in a list, so other people can compare your list with theirs. It's all random. In a parallel universe I could just as easily have become someone else altogether.*

*And, let's face it: everyone lies. We say we like reading, when the only thing we've read in months is* Heat *magazine. We say we're sporty, when we moan if we have to run for the bus. We claim to to be fans of the cool new band, when we've only heard that single from the advert. If we were honest, our profiles would read like this: goes to school, watches TV, texts mates, eats chocolate, picks nose in secret, sleeps a lot. But nobody says that. So we're all liars. So I've got nothing to feel guilty about. Not really.*

It was surprising how easy it was to create my new identity. A doddle. All I needed was one of those free email addresses and a bit of imagination. That Saturday afternoon, I waited until Katie had gone home to do it. She wanted to stick around and help – once she'd realised she couldn't talk me out of it – but I made her leave. I knew if we collaborated we'd just end up dissolving into giggles and coming up with a ridiculous name like Ermintrude Heffelhump. The name I chose had to be believable, simple, and inconspicuous. The new me had to be someone anybody might know – the girl who always sits at the back of the classroom or who sometimes goes to your youth club. She couldn't have any strange hobbies, which might draw attention to her, and she must not have achieved anything which would make her stand out, or worse, anything which could be double-checked. At the same time, she had to be interesting enough to make her an attractive prospect as a friend. She had to be a little older than me, so Alex thought of her as an equal. And, most important, she had to like football, so she had something in common with Alex.

I remembered having seen one of those baby naming books in the spare room and went and fetched it. Some of the names the book suggested were a joke. I mean, seriously, who would call their baby Aldis? Someone who loved their local supermarket? And you've got to really hate your kid to lumber him with Boris, or Cedric.

I played around with names for hours, but I found a good reason for rejecting everything I came up with. Once I'd added a made-up surname, they either sounded like minor members of the Royal Family (Victoria Hermitage) or characters from a sketch show (Isla White). The more I said them aloud, the less they felt like they belonged to me. In the end, I just plumped for the plainest sounding name I could think of: Laura Thompson. It was un-exotic, dependable, a bit mousey. It would do.

She may have had a boring sounding name but, I decided, in other respects Laura would be a lot like me. It would prevent any embarrassing slip-ups. She too would be a Gemini. She'd also have a younger brother who she liked to pretend didn't exist, and a best friend named Katie. She'd have been to the same places as me on holiday, she would have the same ambitions (in other words, be just as clueless about what she wanted to do) and she'd also have a phobia of flying insects, the type that come at you with their big, buggy eyes and dart around your face frantically. The key difference between us would be that she wouldn't have a boyfriend called Jack. Hers would be named Jared, so that if I ever spoke to her and started saying 'Ja—' I could check myself in time and end '. . . red' instead. Katie thought that bit was genius, when I rang to tell her.

I set up a profile page for Laura and pasted in a blurry picture, which Dad had taken on holiday in Turkey, last summer. I was sitting on a horse (a first), my hair was tied up in a ponytail, which I rarely did at home, and I was atypically tanned. If any of my friends came across the profile by accident, it would be easy to persuade them that Laura Thompson just looked a lot like me. It was uncanny. How we'd laugh at the coincidence.

If 'Laura' was to be convincing, she couldn't just be a profile page; she'd need some friends. Obviously, they couldn't be any of my real friends, even Katie, who was in on my plan. It was important that there were no links between Laura and Lily, so nobody could follow the trail and figure out what I'd done. I trawled Topfriendz for suitable candidates, girls of around my age who I had something tenuous in common with, but whom I was never likely to meet, and fired off about fifty friendship request messages, all of which said pretty much the same thing: 'Hi, I'm new to Topfriendz and a massive fan of (insert band name / actor here). It would be great to chat.' I picked a few random guys too, based purely on their looks, I'm ashamed to admit, but if this wasn't a time to be shallow, when was? And finally, feeling very mischievous indeed, I asked Igor – he of the *I want to make talk* line – if he wanted to be Laura's friend. I hoped it would make up for the pain of being rejected by Lily earlier in the day.

Within a couple of hours, Laura had twenty-six friends, including one very happy Igor, and people had even started approaching her with friend requests. I think people just like collecting names to bump up their numbers, in the same way that kids collect stickers. Only a few people rejected Laura, but, strangely, that hurt my pride as much as if they'd rejected me.

By the time I'd added some applications, like games and pointless quizzes (I deliberately ignored the ones that asked 'Are you a good friend?' or 'What's your friendship style?'), there was no way anybody could tell that Laura's page wasn't a genuine one. I'd almost made her flesh and blood. I decided I would grow to like having her around, in spite of her weird fondness for football. She'd be the twin sister I never had, or my imaginary friend, like little kids invent when they're lonely. Except, I wouldn't talk to her aloud. Obviously.

I called Katie with the good news. 'I've done it,' I said, excitedly. 'Have a look. It's Laura Thompson.'

'Hang on,' she said, and I heard her typing in the background. 'Hey, it looks cool. It's such a shame I can't be Laura's friend. She's *such* an inspiration.'

'Stop being sarcastic, Katie. And if you even try making her your friend I'll report you to the moderators.'

'Ha!' Katie snorted. 'That should be interesting.'

'Do you think it looks good enough so that I can contact Alex now?'

'Definitely,' said Katie. 'It really does make you wonder how many of the people on Topfriendz are who they say they are.' She paused, as if she was mentally scrolling down her list of friends and wondering who was an imposter. Then her voice became uncharacteristically serious. 'Lily, for the very last time, I promise, I have to ask you this: are you sure you want to go ahead with this?'

'Yes,' I said. 'One hundred per cent sure.' Which was a lie, because I was only about ninety-nine per cent sure. The other one per cent – call it my conscience – was still niggling a little.

'Do it now, then, while I'm on the phone.'

'OK.' I put Alex's name into the search engine and the profile Katie and I had been looking at earlier reloaded. Nothing had changed; Alex hadn't logged on in the meantime. She was still smiling prettily, oblivious to the predator about to pounce. 'I'm in!' I said. My heart was beating very fast, as if I was about to jet off into space rather than merely generate an online friendship. 'OK, I'm going to write a message . . . I'm typing . . .'

'What are you writing?' Katie asked breathlessly. 'Tell me!'

'I'm saying how great it is to meet another girl who's such a huge football fan and that I think we once played in the same girls' tournament when we were little.'

'You're unbelievable. You don't know anything about football.'

'Nah, but how hard can it be to understand? Boys like it, after all.'

'True. Have you sent it yet?'

'No,' I said. 'Three . . . two . . . one . . . send!' I let go of the return button and the friend request shot off into cyberspace, vanishing into an invisible universe of binary code and other things I don't understand. 'Stage one complete. Now I just have to hope she wants to be my friend.'

'Good luck,' Katie said. 'And let me know the second you hear back from her!'

'I will do,' I said. 'Don't you worry.'

I sat by my computer for a while, staring at Laura's profile and waiting for something to happen. Mum called up from downstairs: 'What are you doing, Lily?'

'I'm just on my computer,' I shouted back. I heard her coming up the stairs.

'You're not on one of those networking sites again, are you?' she asked, from the landing. My door was ajar – the way my parents prefer it, as they think I can't get up to much mischief if they can walk in at will. How naive parents can be. She peered at me through the opening. 'I do worry about the amount of time you spend on that computer. There are all kinds of strange people who prey on young girls like you. It was on the news – those sites can be dangerous.'

'I know, Mum,' I said. 'Don't worry.'

She asked me to put a load of washing on for her. It was mainly made up of Dad's work shirts, crisp white cotton ones with stiff collars and folded-over cuffs. After I'd switched on the machine I stood and watched it for a few moments. I might have imagined it, but I could have sworn that as each shirt began to spin around it raised one sleeve and pointed an accusatory cuff at me.

# Chapter 4

Perhaps this is a good time to explain what I mean when I said that Jack was perfect. I don't mean he was perfect in a genetically modified, Ken doll way; there was nothing plastic about him. His teeth weren't especially even or glowing white, and he had this swirly, whirly bit at the back of his head where his hair would never lie flat, however much gel he layered on it. I'd spent enough time studying his face at microscopic proximity to know that one of his eyes was a little bit larger than the other and that his left nostril was slightly bigger and more triangular than the right. When he grinned, one side of his mouth came up higher than the other. I appreciate I'm now – rather unfairly – drawing a picture of him in which he resembles the Elephant Man following a nasty encounter with an electric socket, but that's what happens when you take a person's features in isolation.

If you've ever looked at anyone's face really closely you'll know that no one is completely symmetrical. I'm not: I have one eyebrow that's more arched than the other (although that could be the result of over-enthusiastic plucking) and a very slightly uneven top lip. So, while Jack was far from a monster, he wasn't Brad Pitt either. On a scale of one to ten (one being hideous gargoyle and ten the aforementioned Mr Pitt), I'd give him an eight. Too good for me, I know; I'm only a six. I've read that if you want to have a lasting relationship you're supposed to go out with people who are at a similar level of attractiveness to you, which means I should have felt permanently insecure in the knowledge that at some point Jack would realise his mistake and leave me for someone better-looking. Which I didn't, because he always made me feel like I was a ten. Which, itself, was one of the reasons why he was perfect.

What else? Let me see. He had perfect manners – in the opening the door for you, always calling when he said he would way – and I could tell he did it because he wanted to, not just because he knew he should. He was funny, without being a clown, and knowledgeable without being cocky. He listened to me, even when I was rambling on and on about nothing, but he wasn't monosyllabic in response, like some boys. He was kind about my friends, polite to my parents and really sweet with my little brother. But he wasn't sickeningly nice: he'd been known to play wicked practical jokes on people, like removing all the furniture from his sister's room while she was out, and setting it up again in the garage, in exactly the same order. It was way before my time, but I don't think she found it very amusing. Then again, I did say he was the perfect boyfriend, not the perfect brother.

It seems weird to think now, but I wasn't at all sure Jack would call after the party. He'd taken my number, yes, and he'd promised he would use it but, in my experience, a boy storing your number in his phone doesn't always equate to him actually dialling it. I wondered if Jack would get home, sleep on it and decide he hadn't liked me all that much after all. Or, his sister might say of me, 'She wasn't all that,' and he'd think better of his instinct to call. Or, he could just chicken out altogether.

Call me contrary, but while I hoped he would call, I didn't want him to call too soon. Everyone knows there are rules about these things. Sunday – the day after – would have been far too early, making him look desperate. But Thursday would have been too late; by then I'd have convinced myself he wasn't interested and made myself get over him, and I'd have made my weekend plans. That left an open window of three days. Three days of constant phone checking. Three days of butterflies in my tummy. Three days of daydreaming.

I simply can't imagine how people ever got together in the old days before texting and instant messaging and email. Before people even had mobile phones, when they used two cups and a bit of string. OK, that last bit isn't true. My mum told me that when she met a guy, he'd have to call her house and risk her parents answering, which of course led to loads of embarrassing questions. When they did get to speak, she couldn't be certain her parents weren't listening in from another extension but, even if they weren't, she could be sure that after about twenty minutes they'd be shouting at her to get off the phone so they could use it. With technology being so limited, sometimes my mum and her boyfriends actually wrote letters to each other, like people in Jane Austen books. Can you believe that? I've no idea how anybody ever dated properly. It's a wonder I was even born.

Jack rang on Tuesday. He sent a brief text first, saying hi and how lovely it was to have met me, and did I want to meet up. It pinged into my inbox at seven o'clock, during dinner. I left it for about half an hour before I replied, mainly because we were having apple crumble for dessert as a treat, and I didn't want to miss out. I was suddenly ravenous. I hadn't eaten much the previous few days – all those pesky butterflies flapping around don't leave much room for food – and knowing Jack was interested in going out with me after all brought my appetite back in an instant. Once I'd virtually licked my plate clean, I excused myself from the table, went up to my room and texted him back. Two minutes later, my phone began to ring. I took a deep breath before answering, so my voice wasn't shaky or too high.

'Hello?'

'Hi Lily, it's Jack.' He didn't sound at all nervous, but

33

some people are good at hiding it. 'I wondered if you were free on Friday. Maybe we could go out for a pizza or something.'

'Sure,' I said, trying to conceal my delight with nonchalance. 'I'd like that.' I wasn't just trying to appear cool, I figured that if I didn't speak much, I'd be less likely to say something stupid. I didn't know Jack well enough to have a proper conversation and I didn't want to labour over smalltalk.

'So I'll pick you up at seven then.'

'Sure, that's fine.' Just in case I sounded a bit too blasé, I added: 'I'm looking forward to it.'

'Me too,' he said.

After that, I gave him my address and the directions to my house, which doesn't bear repeating. I'm only pointing it out because it bugs me how in TV shows and movies people make dates but never finalise the arrangements. They say things like 'I'll meet you for a drink at Ed's', without specifying the time, or 'Pick me up', without saying where they live. In films, no one ever has to spell their address or explain that they live in a flat with a dodgy doorbell so it's best to knock hard instead, and ooh, mind the dog. People in movies just seem to arrive in places together magnetically. Maybe they're all telepathic. In real life, people need maps and timetables.

We didn't speak again, and by the time Friday came I could barely remember anything about Jack except that I'd liked him when we'd met at the party. I couldn't even picture his face. 'I hope I recognise him,' I told Katie. 'What if he turns up at the door and I don't fancy him any more?'

She laughed at me. 'Yeah, and what if he doesn't fancy you? Come to think of it, he might not turn up at all!'

'You're so mean,' I said. 'Which is partly why I love you.'

I needn't have worried. A few minutes before seven, I heard a car parking outside. I looked out of my bedroom window and saw Jack's instantly recognisable and attractive silhouette loitering at my garden gate, clearly biding his time so he didn't arrive too early. I felt a pang of nervousness and put on another layer of lip-gloss. When he rang the doorbell, I hung about upstairs and allowed my parents to let him in, so they could check him over and conclude for themselves that he was respectable enough to date their daughter. We'd already been through the 'Are you sure he's not too old for you?' discussion, which was prompted by Katie's comment about his car. It wasn't the age difference that bothered them, but the fear I'd end up wrapped around a lamp post.

'We're only going out for pizza,' I'd assured them. 'I wouldn't go joy-riding until at least the third date.'

I listened from the landing for a couple of minutes to make sure things were going well, then made my appearance at the top of the stairs before Mum and Dad could ask him too many probing questions. Jack gave me a quick glance as I came down. He breathed an almost audible sigh of relief, but I couldn't tell if was because he thought I scrubbed up OK, or just because he'd be able to stop making polite conversation with my parents.

'Ah, here she is,' said Dad, in the tone of voice you'd use to present someone to the Queen. His eyes went straight to my skirt and I could tell he was using a mental tape measure to work out if it was long enough.

Mum smiled at me. 'You two have a good night,' she said, nodding approvingly at Jack. 'And remember, drive carefully and don't be home too late.'

'We'll be waiting up,' said Dad, his warm tone masking the veiled threat.

Whatever Katie may have told Dad, Jack doesn't, in fact, drive a Vauxhall Astra. On our first date I discovered that he owns a battered old green Beetle, one of those retro cars that has round edges and looks a bit like it's smiling at you. It's rickety and bumpy and stalls a lot. It's the sort of car people say has 'character', which really means that it's ugly and ancient. Jack told me his uncle gave it to him when he passed his test.

We didn't go anywhere fancy, just the local pizza restaurant, which was cheap and cheerful and somewhere we both felt at home. Jack said I could order whatever I wanted, which I took to mean he was paying. In the past I'd have got a salad from the 'all you can eat' salad bar, but somebody had recently told me that there are billions of bacteria in all the salads because people go to the loo and don't wash their hands, and then stick their fingers in, which is so gross it put me off for ever. Plus, it turns out that all the oily dressings mean there are just as many calories in the salads as there are in a pizza. When I relayed this to Jack, he said that sometimes you're better off not knowing too much. But I did notice that he didn't have a side salad.

I ordered a pizza with mushrooms and Jack had one with anchovies and olives. He was easy company; I could be one hundred per cent myself and chatting to him felt as natural as talking to Katie, although we weren't as rude to each other, obviously. I wondered whether the way Jack ate his pizza said anything about him and whether it meant we were compatible. I always start from the inside out, leaving the empty circle of the crust on my plate. Jack ate his way around his pizza in a clockwise direction, as if he was consuming a clock, hour by hour. He caught me staring at him and put down his fork. 'Are you OK, Lily?'

'I'm great,' I said. I didn't want him to think I was the sort of person who analyses the way people eat pizza, even though I am. Not on the very first date. 'I guess I've just got order envy.'

'Here,' he said, cutting me a neat little triangle of his pizza and placing it on his fork. 'Try some.'

He leaned in towards me, holding his fork to my mouth, and there was a brief moment of awkwardness when we both realised that this was exactly the kind of clichéd romantic thing couples do on a date. It reminded me of the kiss we hadn't yet enjoyed, the kiss that, hopefully, would come later.

'Mmm,' I said, lying – literally – through my teeth, as I bit into the pizza. I hate anchovies. I think they taste like salty worms, although I've never actually eaten a salty worm, so I can't be sure.

'Do you want to swap?'

'No, no, that's very chivalrous of you, but I'm fine with my mushroom, honestly.' And, I thought, chuckling to myself, you're already a 'fungi' to be with – although I'd never have dared say anything that cheesy (ha!) aloud.

It's just as well that I didn't say it, or I'd have ruined what happened next. Jack must have been thinking exactly the same as me (about the kiss, not the mushrooms) because he looked directly into my eyes, put his knife and fork down and took my hands in his. Then he snogged me right there and then, in the middle of the restaurant, not caring who was watching. It was amazing, even if his mouth did taste a bit salty. He moved his chair so that it was next to mine and we kissed until the cheese on the pizza had grown so cold it curled up and turned to rubber. And when the restaurant staff started stacking up all the chairs, Jack paid the bill and took me home.

# chapter 5

♡

It was on our first date that I learned not only what a great kisser Jack was, but also how cagey he could be about certain aspects of his life. To start with, I thought he was a just a very good listener. That's on the checklist of 'qualities to look for in a boyfriend' in every magazine I've ever read, so I ticked it off, happily. He wanted to know all about my friends, my schoolwork, my family, what films I liked, music, the books I'd read, everything.

As the evening went on, I started to think that maybe he was *too* good a listener. Much as I like talking about myself, I wanted to know about him too. And in that respect, he was a lot less generous. He was happy to tell me all about his karate classes (it turned out that was the type of martial art he did – apparently, it's all about discipline and self-control and other stuff that sounds no fun at all) and his college and his new friends, but when it came to anything more personal, he didn't have much to say. It was almost as if he'd learnt and rehearsed a set of answers, and he couldn't deviate from them. Even asking the most basic, obvious questions made me feel I was prying. He'd deflect everything back to me, as though we were playing tennis with facts.

'How come you moved here?'

'My mum got a new job.' No pause for breath. 'What does your mum do?'

'She's a nurse. So are your parents divorced?'

'No, my dad died.'

'Oh, I'm so sorry, Jack. When?'

'When I was twelve.' No emotion. 'Have you always lived here?'

'Yes, since I was born. That's awful, Jack, you must really miss him.'

'Not really. I hardly remember him. Your parents seem cool, for parents. Do you get on with them?'

And so on. It was frustrating and not a little bit weird. I justified it to myself, thinking he must be a private person and that things I could talk about as openly as what I had for breakfast were simply harder for him to reveal. Then he kissed me, and I discovered a much more pleasurable way of getting to know him better. It's amazing how kissing someone can make you forget all your niggles, for a while at least, and how it can make you feel you know them inside out, even when you don't.

On our second date, we went to the cinema, so there wasn't much time for talking – and the people in the row behind us would have had something to say about it. By our third date, when we went bowling, we'd been talking on the phone for an hour every night and my state of continued ignorance was starting to nark me. I planned to have it out with Jack the next time I saw him. But as soon as I opened the front door to him for our fourth date (ice skating), some sort of chemical reaction occurred which made me feel too into Jack to think anything other than, 'Wow, you are so gorgeous' (when I wasn't thinking, 'Arghh, I'm going flying'). I'm not making excuses, honestly. I'd just look at him and my stomach would fall into my feet.

By our fifth date, a burger and chips followed by a DVD at my house, we were beginning to slot into the routine of each other's daily lives and had gone beyond those sorts of basic 'getting to know you' questions altogether. There comes a point when, if you've grown close to someone, you feel you can't ask certain things because you believe you should already know the answers. It's embarrassing. It's like not knowing how many brothers and sisters your best mate has, or realising you don't know the colour of your boyfriend's eyes. It shows you haven't been paying attention, that you're a bad friend or a rubbish girlfriend. So you stop asking.

Of course that doesn't mean my questions went away. Sometimes, I'd completely forget about them for a while and then something would happen to make me think of them again. Jack might let a new detail slip out – Alex's surname, for example, when he was talking about a football match he'd been to – and it would get me wondering. Instead of pestering Jack with my questions, I decided to discuss them with Katie instead. It wasn't long before she began to come up with all her crazy theories about his past. She thought she was being funny, that it was all a game and that I was, as usual, creating a drama out of nothing, and so the more I questioned, the wilder her fantasies became: maybe Jack's family were in a witness protection programme; maybe he killed his dad; maybe his dad was a famous Hollywood actor because, well, Jack did look a teeny bit like Matt Damon, didn't he? I'd laugh along with Katie, but a little part of me would wonder if there really was something dark or dodgy in Jack's past.

Whenever you hear about serial killers on the news, there are always interviews with neighbours and friends who say, 'But he seemed like such a nice guy' or, 'He was perfectly ordinary' and, 'Nobody would have guessed'. Some of them have jobs and girlfriends whom they go home to every night, and they'll do the washing up and watch soaps together. A person can be charming and have perfect manners and still be a monster.

Now, I'm not saying that I ever thought Jack might have been a serial killer, because that would be crazy, stupid and totally ridiculous, but it makes you think, doesn't it?

# Chapter 6

♡

*I did it for both of us. For me and for Jack. I thought that if I knew everything about him, if I didn't have any more unanswered questions, then we could be properly happy. Not knowing was stopping me from falling absolutely in love with him. If he hadn't been so secretive, I wouldn't have needed to involve Alex, would I?*

*Sometimes I wonder if I wasn't the only one who created a new identity to get what I wanted. I only changed my name and a couple of little details, but Jack totally reinvented himself, packing up all the memories he didn't want to share in sealed boxes and then putting them in storage somewhere. He hardly kept in touch with any of his old friends, and he sure as hell didn't want me to meet them. He steered me away from his mum – I'd only met her to say hello or goodbye to – and when I asked to see photos of him as a child, or with his dad, he said he didn't have any. Who doesn't keep pictures of their dead dad?*

*How could I believe him when he said how much he liked me, when his own dad meant so little to him? How could I be sure he felt anything at all?*

It was almost two whole weeks after I'd sent my message that I heard back from Alex. Scrub that. What I really mean is that it was nearly two whole weeks before Laura heard back from Alex. Being two people can get quite confusing – sometimes even I couldn't remember who I was at a given moment. During that icy, bleak January fortnight, when it was too cold and too dark to do anything else, I went on Topfriendz more than I ever had before, every morning before school and the second I arrived home, after dinner and before bed. I rarely bothered checking my own profile, only Laura's. Each time I logged in, I hoped for a 'You've got a new friend' confirmation and, if I was lucky, even a message from Alex. Instead, what I received were several friend requests (ironically, Laura seemed to be far more popular than Lily ever was), a 'Hello lovely laydee' from Igor, and an invitation to a gig by some band called The Wonderfulls. The lead singer was quite cute, but their angsty Emo music wasn't my – or Laura's – thing at all. I like music you can dance to, not music that makes you want to slit your wrists.

I began to convince myself that Alex wasn't going to get in touch, doubting myself for ever coming up with such a stupid scheme. Why, I asked myself, would she be interested in becoming my 'friend', when she already had loads of friends – real friends? And even if she did accept my friend request, it was likely nothing more would come of it. Laura would just take her place as another name in a long list of names, there to make up the numbers. There was no reason why Alex should reply, she probably had a very busy life, what with her A-levels and her football and her mates. To her, Topfriendz was almost certainly nothing more than a diversion, something you join because everyone else does, just as it had been for me. Maybe I should have seen her silence as a sign: 'Quit while you're ahead. Don't go there. It was a bad idea and you've had a lucky escape. Get out now, while you still can.' Gosh, there are a lot of expressions that mean virtually the same thing, aren't there?

The only thing that didn't cross my mind, as I tortured myself with all the what-ifs and the maybes and the buts, was the possibility that Alex might not go on Topfriendz every day, the fact she hadn't even seen my message yet. But I've never been one to let logic get in the way of paranoia.

So, when I logged on, one Thursday evening, to see alerts telling me that I not only had one new friend, but also a message from Alex Porter, it came as a surprise. A very pleasant surprise. I was so excited I almost shouted out 'Alex has got back to Laura!', which would have made everyone in my family think that I was on some sort of covert spying mission in my bedroom, exchanging secrets with the Russians in code. Or, more likely, that I'd finally lost the plot

45

altogether. I hesitated about whether to call Katie before opening the message, so we could read it together, but I'd just put some fake tan on my face, one of those little sample sachets that comes free in a magazine, and I didn't want it to rub off all over my phone and go streaky.

Tentatively, my heart bumping away in my chest as if I'd had three Red Bulls, I opened Alex's message. This is what it said:

*Hi Laura.*

*How's it going? Good to hear from you. I think I do vaguely remember you from that sports camp when I was ten. Are you still playing? It's great to talk to another girl who's into football. None of my college mates are, I think they think I'm a bit weird, to be honest. What team do you support? I'm a huge Arsenal fan. Don't say you support Spurs, or I'll delete you from my friend list! LOL! It would be good to chat to you again. What are you up to these days?*

*Love Alex xx*

Result! I couldn't have hoped for more. Alex was friendly, she wanted me to write back and she seemed really keen to get to know me better. She even thought she remembered me! It's amazing what people will say so they don't seem rude or ignorant; they will even convince themselves that a complete fabrication is the truth, rewriting history in the process. Alex probably spent hours racking her brains, wading through the fog of her distant memories, trying to put Laura's name and face on to the body of a little ten-year-old girl whom she met at some stupid kids' summer camp years ago. She wiped that poor girl's identity and replaced it with mine (Laura's). She concluded that I was someone she had once known.

So excited that I could barely steady my hands to type, I texted Katie:

*OMG K! Alex msgd!*

*OMG!!* came her reply. And then a moment later: *Call me!*

*I cnt*, I texted back. *Fk tan is wet.*

It can't have been more than ten seconds later that my phone started ringing. I put it straight on to loudspeaker.

'Oh my God, Lil,' Katie shouted. 'You can't use fake tan as an excuse not to tell me the most exciting thing that's happened in weeks!'

'You wouldn't understand,' I told her, as my own voice echoed back at me through the speaker. 'You don't need to use it. Your skin is all lovely and golden brown all year round, already.'

'OK, OK,' she said. 'So I don't get fake tan. For God's sake tell me what Alex said!'

'It's mad. She actually thinks she remembers me.'

'No! How come? What else did she say?'

'She asked me which football team I support and said it was good to talk to another girl who's into football. I told you football was the line to go with, didn't I? She wants me to write back.' I read Katie the message, so she knew as much as me about Alex.

'Ah, she sounds really nice. Are you going to write back? Are you going to ask her about Jack?'

'Don't be a zombie, Kay, I can't just steam on in there and say, "Hi Alex, good to hear from you and, by the way, it's not just an interest in football that we've got in common."'

'I know that,' said Katie, sounding hurt. 'I was only wondering.'

'Sure, hon. But I think I need to get to know her a bit before I ask any probing questions.'

'So what are you going to say?'

'I think I'll tell her a little about myself – about Laura. I'll ask her a few questions too, so she has to write back, and then take it from there. If I treat the whole thing like I've just made a new friend, and I'm getting to know her, like I'd get to know any new friend, I reckon she won't suspect a thing.'

Making a new friend was, to all intents and purposes, exactly what I was doing – if you ignore the fact that the friendship was built on slightly dubious foundations (a nicer term for lies), and that my motives weren't exactly pure. I genuinely didn't know much about Alex at all, save her name and the fact she'd once gone out with Jack, so it wasn't as if I was going to have to pretend to be ignorant about her. If I'd met her in different circumstances, she could have been someone I might choose to be friends with. Jack liked her, and Jack liked me, so we must have some qualities in common.

Was I using her? No more so than many people use their friends. Why do people make friends with each other anyway? They do it because they want to be in the cool clique, or because they're lonely, or because they want to show someone else how interesting and how much fun they are. Everybody uses each other to a certain extent, even if it's just to have someone to go shopping with.

I wrote back to Alex later that evening. I said it was great that she remembered me from camp but, no, I wasn't playing football any more. Was she? And wasn't it a coincidence that she was an Arsenal fan because, guess what, so was I! All I really knew about Arsenal was that they were a north London team, which made them my local team. But I knew I could get some more information out of Jack about them, if I needed to. I asked her what A-levels she was doing and told her I was doing my AS-levels that summer – thereby making myself (or Laura) skip a whole year like a total brainbox, when I hadn't even chosen my options yet. She couldn't know I was a full two years younger than her, or she might think I was some kid with a crush. I didn't think we'd still be in touch by the summer, when I had to take my dreaded GCSEs, so it didn't really matter. I signed off my message with three kisses, even though she'd only put two. But who's counting?

I read my message three times before I sent it, to make sure there weren't any slip-ups, like accidentally writing my own name instead of Laura's, or mentioning Jack. You know when you're not supposed to think about something, so you

49

can't stop thinking about it? It's like being on a diet and craving chocolate all the time, when if you weren't dieting you'd only want it a couple of times a week. The whole time I was writing to Alex I couldn't stop thinking about Jack, so much so that I initially wrote, 'I jacked in playing football,' which isn't even an expression I'd normally use. That was the guilt typing for me, I guess. It was probably also guilt that, a few minutes after I'd sent the message, made me call Jack and tell him I was missing him, even though we'd spoken only an hour earlier.

# Chapter 7

♡

Once we'd started writing to each other, Alex and I fell into a pattern of messaging or emailing at least a couple of times a week. She'd tell me what she'd been doing and I'd tell her whatever I decided Laura had been up to that day, which was usually what I'd done, with a bit of embellishment. The key to telling a good lie, someone once told me, is to make it as close to the truth as possible, so your stories ring true and you're less likely to slip up, or forget what you've said. Laura was ninety-nine per cent me; she talked like me and she thought like me. The differences were just fine print, the tiny type at the bottom of the page that no one reads when they download a ringtone or enter a competition.

When it came to Jared, on the other hand, the fictional boyfriend of my alter ego, I could be as inventive as I liked. The less he was like Jack, the better. Jared, I decided, was dark and skinny, and he was the bass player in a band. Part of the reason for this lie was that Jack is tone deaf, so I thought it would throw Alex off the scent, if she ever grew suspicious. Plus, I've always kind of liked the idea of having a boyfriend who played in a band.

What surprised me most about the whole charade was how natural it felt to chat to Alex; it was like getting to know any new friend. Although, if I'm honest, I probably made more effort with her than I would usually make with a person I didn't know that well, especially someone I met on Topfriendz. If she didn't write for a while, I wouldn't let things drift, or start getting paranoid wondering what I'd done to offend her: my typical responses. I'd just send her another message.

I think growing a friendship is a bit like looking after a goldfish. For a while, it's perfectly happy to swim around in a bowl on its own, eating the crumbs you throw its way. But, if you forget to feed it for a while, or don't change the water, one day you come home from school and it's just floating on the top. Dead.

I've always been fantastic at making new friends, but not so good at keeping them. (I'm rubbish at keeping goldfish too; Dad banned me from having any more.) Staying in touch with people I meet and then don't see regularly is such an effort. When I was younger, the friendships I made at summer camps usually only lasted until I returned to school in September. Life just gets in the way and, after a few months, unless you keep chatting, you go right back to being strangers. It's hard enough keeping up with your best mates, let alone people you've met once or twice, or have shared a couple of weeks' holiday with.

Making the effort with Alex was different because it was a means to an end, a project. At least, that's how it started. Sometimes, when we were chatting, I almost forgot about what I'd set out to do. The truth is, I hadn't expected to like her as much as I did, or to enjoy the process of getting to know her. I'd intended to steam in, take the information I was after and get straight out, but I couldn't do that. Alex was sweet and funny and kind. When I told her Jared had trapped his hand in a car door (a story I made up to curtail his bass playing for a while, after she started asking too many questions about his band's gigs), she remembered to keep asking how he was recovering, when his bandages were coming off, and so on. She was always thoughtful, even though her life seemed so much fuller than mine. As well as college and her football, she did drama and she even volunteered at an old people's home. I felt so boring in comparison, with my dearth of hobbies, that I told her I played the violin (I had a few lessons when I was eleven) and had once been selected to represent the county at gymnastics (yeah, right).

The only difficult part of chatting to Alex was negotiating the subject of football without slipping up. God, it was boring. I'd sold myself as an expert – a former player as well as a fan – but I was as ignorant about football as I am about brain surgery. This is the sum total of what I knew about it: a bunch of fit men in shorts run around a pitch for an incredibly long time kicking a ball into a net. Some of them have nice legs and stupid haircuts. Some of them advertise stuff on TV. They all have incredibly glamorous wives and girlfriends, with fake tans and too much bling. Put it this way: if *Match of the Day* were looking for a new presenter, this knowledge would probably not have got me the job.

On several occasions, being a football dunce almost landed me in trouble.

*Did you see that goal?* Alex messaged one evening, after there had been some big cup match on TV.

*Which goal?* I replied, trying to keep my options open.

*Duh. There was only one goal! The one that Ronaldo scored.*

*Only kidding. Yes, it was awesome.*

*What? Sometimes I wonder who you support! The referee was having a laugh. It was so offside it wasn't true. Don't you think?*

*Yes,* I agreed. I had no idea what offside meant and guessed it was some new sort of exclamatory term, like phat or sick but for football. *It was totally offside* I continued. *It was so off its side it was practically horizontal.*

*LOL. You have a really strange way of looking at things, Laura.*

I'd got away with it again. Funny how idiocy can sometimes masquerade as charm.

Whenever Alex brought up football, I longed to change the subject. But I knew I mustn't. Tedious as it was, football was the deal-clincher, the supposed shared interest that had made her warm to me in the first place. Aware that my ignorance was going to give me away eventually, I accepted that I had to do something about it: I needed to learn about the 'beautiful game', as my dad calls it (no wonder he needs glasses). I tried the web, but I couldn't understand a word on the fan sites, and the news reports were so dull that reading them made me suicidal. I knew my best option was to ask Jack, even though I felt a teensy bit bad about doing it.

'Can I ask you something about football?' I said to him, on the evening of my 'offside discussion' with Alex.

'Sure,' he said, sounding bemused. 'Fire away.'

'What exactly does offside mean?'

He laughed at me, which I wasn't expecting. Clearly, this offside thing was something everybody is supposed to know, like how to boil an egg. 'Lily, you are such a female cliché. I can't believe you're asking me that. OK, basically, it's when the . . .'

I'm afraid I can't remember a single word he said, until, 'Since when have you got interested in football?'

'Oh, you know . . . I was talking to my dad and ended up watching a bit of the match with him and I quite enjoyed it.' For extra impact, I added, 'That Ronaldo goal was so offside!'

'It sure was,' he said, and I could tell he was grinning. 'I really like that you're getting into football. Although I have to say, I'm a bit surprised.'

'Oh, I'm full of surprises,' I said, and for a moment I really hated myself.

The consequence of telling Jack that I had suddenly developed an interest in football was that he now insisted on talking to me about it at every opportunity. I hadn't been aware how much he loved it, in the same way as I'd loved the Spice Girls when I was a little kid. He was a super fan; he couldn't get enough of it. Talking about it made him sound excitable and knowledgeable and happy, which was kind of cute, if I could have taken away the football part.

Even worse than having to talk about football was having to watch it. If I happened to be seeing Jack and there was a football match on TV, he'd suggest that we see it together, and I had to feign enthusiasm. He found most matches so riveting that he didn't even want to snog much (and believe me, I tried), except at half time, just in case he missed an important ball.

Katie didn't have any sympathy for me: she laughed and said it was my punishment for what I'd done. 'Sitting through ninety minutes of football is your penance for lying to Alex and to Jack,' she said. I think she was half serious too, but then she was brought up a Catholic.

And, oh, the irony. The result of being forced to watch and talk about football all the time was that, even against my will, I did end up learning quite a lot, so that when I chatted to Alex on Topfriendz, I really did sound like I knew what I was talking about. At the end of the day, it's a game of two halves (that's an in-joke). I can now, fairly convincingly, I believe, tell anyone who asks everything they never wanted to know about a four-four-two formation, a corner kick, and an indirect free kick. I really hope I won't have to.

I knew learning about football would help me grow closer to Alex; that was the idea. What I hadn't expected was that it would also bring Jack closer to me. Now that he believed he could share his love of football, he wanted to see me more often. He even seemed more affectionate (except during matches). It didn't take a genius to work out that he liked me more just because he thought I liked football. At first, that made me feel guiltier than ever, but then it irritated me. It made me see that he'd been holding a part of himself back from me. It also helped me to understand why he had fallen for Alex in such a big way; they were football clones – they even used the same phrases sometimes. I felt jealous that they'd genuinely shared something, when I was just pretending. And that made me even more determined to find out why they'd split up and what else Jack was hiding.

# chapter 8
♡

One February afternoon, about five weeks after I'd first made contact with Alex, I arrived home from school to find an unexpected message waiting in Laura's Topfriendz inbox. This is what it said:

*Hi Laura*

*How do you fancy meeting up? My dad has tickets for the Arsenal game on Saturday, and my uncle can't make it, so there's one going spare. Would you like to come instead? Dad says you don't have to pay and he'll drop us off somewhere so we can have a coffee afterwards. No worries if you're busy or if you don't want to come along, but it would be great to see you. Let me know if you can make it.*

*Love Alex xxxxx*

'Oh my God!' I said aloud, my voice high with panic. 'She wants to meet me.' And then I thought, Of course she does, because that's what normal people who have become friends online do. Because Alex doesn't know this isn't a normal friendship. I know I must sound seriously dense, but of all the scenarios I'd imagined, the possibility of meeting Alex in the flesh was not one of them; it hadn't crossed my mind. Obviously, I hadn't thought things through at all.

Meeting Alex face to face presented an entirely new set of problems. It would mean taking Laura out of the safety of my bedroom, where she was confined to a computer screen, and presenting her to the world as a real flesh and blood human being. It would mean being her for a whole afternoon, not just for a few minutes at a time. It would mean selling myself as someone else, not only to Alex, but to her dad. What if I slipped up? What if I bumped into someone I knew and they called me by my real name? What if Alex met me and decided she didn't like me after all? All my work would have been wasted. And what on earth would I say to Jack? I'd have to make up a story about where I was going, pretend I was with someone else, somewhere else. I'd be taking my betrayal to another level altogether, no longer just omitting to tell him something, but actively telling him a huge, whopping, dirty lie because he could never, ever find out the truth: that I was meeting his ex-girlfriend behind his back.

I laughed, one of those nervous, off-key laughs that isn't

about anything being funny. The idea was ridiculous. I couldn't go to the match with Alex. It was too risky. But what possible reason could Laura have for not wanting to meet Alex, when they were getting on so well? Wouldn't she be squealing with excitement at the prospect of going to see her favourite football team play? My football knowledge might have been limited, but I did know that football tickets were really expensive and hard to get – Jack was always going on about it. He'd have killed for Alex's spare ticket.

I had no idea what to do. I sat staring at the screen, while the cursor blinked furiously at me. Go on, it dared. Blink. Make a decision. Write back to Alex. She'll know you're home now and will have read her message. She's waiting for you. Go on. Blink.

Hard as I tried, I couldn't make up my mind what to do. I toyed with a few possible responses:

*I'd love to come,* I typed. *Unfortunately, we're going on holiday on Friday. And* I wanted to add, *we're never coming back.* Delete.

*I would have liked to come but I have terrible toothache and Saturday afternoon is the only time I can get an appointment with the dentist.* Delete.

*I'd love to meet you, but I might have forgotten to mention that I have this embarrassing skin condition that makes me come out in great, big puss-filled boils, and the doctor says it might be contagious.* Delete.

*Did I say I liked football? Well, I lied. And, by the way, my name isn't really Laura, it's Lily. I'm not your friend. I've been using you to get information about your ex-boyfriend.*

Funny how the most outlandish, absurd excuse of all was the true one. Seeing my confession spelled out in black type made me feel sick. I left it sitting on the screen for a while, daring myself to send it, a part of me wanting to send it and end the charade. A little fly – too tiny even to scare me – was buzzing around the room and I wondered what would happen if it landed on the return key and took the decision out of my hands. I watched it as if flew towards me, but as it neared the keyboard it seemed to change its mind and spin around, heading for the window. 'Well, you're no help!' I called after it. 'Useless insect.' Maybe fate could help. I took a coin out of my purse. 'Right, heads I go to the match. Tails I send this message and probably have to leave the country.' It landed tail side up. 'All right, best of three.' Tails again. 'Best of five, then . . .'

In the end, I did what I always do when I can't make a decision on my own: I rang Katie.

'You've got to go,' she said, after repeating, 'Oh my God!' about thirty times, each time sounding a fraction more excited. Her attitude towards my deception had changed since I'd heard back from Alex. Now, she wanted the whole thing over with as quickly as possible. 'You've been messaging each other for weeks and you still haven't found out anything juicy. Meet her and you'll finally be able to get the dirt on Jack.'

I tutted. 'I've told you, I can't just ask her straight out. The subject hasn't come up.' If I sounded irritated, it was because Katie asked me whether Alex had told me anything about Jack yet virtually every time I brought her name up. It was almost as if she wanted to know more than I did. She didn't understand how difficult it was to steer our conversations round to personal things I wasn't even supposed to know about.

'Yeah, but if you meet her, you might get the opportunity to ask. And at least you'll get to know her a bit better.'

'That's true. But I feel really bad about the idea. Talking to someone on the net isn't like real life. I mean, I know it is, but people sort of accept that you're not completely being yourself when you message them, don't they? Everybody is cleverer and funnier and has a better personality online. Everyone lies a bit. If I meet Alex I have to lie to her face and I'll be letting her dad pay for my ticket, and that seems really wrong.'

'Making up Laura in the first place was bad. Pretending to be Alex's friend was bad. Why is meeting her any worse?'

'I guess you're right. It's not worse, it's just more real. So maybe I should just bail out now. I could delete Laura's account, make her disappear, and Alex wouldn't be able to find any trace of her.'

'Pointless. She'd be gutted and you still wouldn't know any more about Jack.'

'Hmm,' I said. 'So I've got to go through with it, then? Shit.'

'Yeah,' said Katie. 'You've got to finish what you started.'

'What about Jack?' I asked. 'What do I tell him? I was supposed to be seeing him Saturday.'

'Just say you've got to meet me and you'll meet him later. Say I needed you to come shopping with me for a dress, or whatever.'

'OK.' I thought for a moment. Maybe there was a way of putting off my decision a little longer. 'You know what? I'm going to call Jack now and get him to come round. I'm going to give him one last chance to tell me everything, and if he does I'll end it with Alex. If he doesn't, I'll tell her I'll go to the match with her.'

'Sounds like a plan,' said Katie. 'Good luck.'

# chapter 9

♡

*I know it was my fault, that nobody made me do it. But if only Jack had made up a decent story about Alex and his dad, instead of being so evasive, then I wouldn't have had to do it. I wouldn't have felt the need to do it. Why didn't he just say, 'Alex dumped me because she met someone else' and make me feel sorry for him? Poor Jack, I'd have thought, what a bitch that Alex was, she so didn't deserve you ... Why didn't he tell me his dad had died in a car accident, or a plane crash, or been knifed outside a pub, or something equally tragic? I wouldn't have asked for the gory details, I'm sure I wouldn't. I'd have swallowed those stories and I'd have been satisfied and I'd probably have cared about him more.*

*Who ever came up with the idea that honesty is always the best policy?*

\* \* \*

My pathetic plan didn't work, which is why I found myself waiting anxiously outside the entrance to Arsenal football ground at two-thirty the following Saturday afternoon. As I stood in the cold, swarms of expectant real fans gathering around me, I felt like a fish out of water, contemplating a terrible fate, which is probably the way my very last goldfish felt when it decided to throw itself out of its bowl in a final act of suicidal desperation. You know those shots in films and adverts where someone is standing completely still, frozen in time, while everything and everyone whirls around them at a double speed? That was me. I was virtually rooted to the spot with fear and anticipation; I think I knew that if I took just one step I'd probably keep on walking until I got all the way home.

Jack had come round the night I received Alex's message, just as I'd intended. Unfortunately, we'd spent most of the evening doing my maths coursework. Saying I needed his help with it was the only way I could persuade my parents to allow him to visit on a school night and, annoyingly, he took me at my word. That's the thing with Jack, he doesn't do hints or subtlety. If you want him to understand what you really mean, you have to spell things out to him in block capitals and, obviously, in this instance, I couldn't. I find that boys are often a bit dense like that. You just have to look at another girl in a particular way and she 'gets' it, without a word being said. But boys? It's like trying to take an x-ray through lead. I suppose it has its advantages. It's certainly much easier to pull the wool over Dad's eyes than Mum's.

Two hours after Jack arrived, we'd endured eating dinner with my parents and we'd listened to a couple of tracks I'd downloaded, but I still hadn't made any headway, either with the matter at hand or with my maths coursework.

'The "x" goes there,' Jack said, showing no signs of impatience whatsoever, despite having explained the equation to me at least eight times. 'See?'

'I think so,' I said. 'Sort of. So the "y" goes there?'

He sighed. 'No, Lil. It goes at the end. Like I showed you before. Y equals five.'

'I still don't get it. We're going to be here all night at this rate.' I pouted. 'Can't you just do it for me, and then we can do something more interesting?'

He smiled and shook his head. 'I could do, but then you still won't understand it and you'll flunk the exam. And then your dad will come after me.'

'I don't care,' I said. 'It's not like I'm ever going to use it in life, is it?'

'You might do. You'll probably use it when you don't even realise it, like when you're shopping or in your job.'

'What?' I giggled to myself. 'Yeah, but only if I'm shopping for a mermaid's underwear. Algae bra! Get it?'

Did I really say that aloud? I must have done because Jack groaned. 'That's terrible. Be serious, Lil. I know maths is a big yawn, but it's kind of necessary. And besides, you've got to pass it so you can move on to Sixth Form. Five more minutes, just for me?'

'God, Jack, you sound like someone's dad. Stop being so sensible.' I looked at my watch. It was nine o'clock. I was running out of time. How could I get him from algebra to Alex?

'Are you calling me boring?'

'Yes, Jack.' I faked a yawn. 'You're turning into a super nerd. Go on then, do it for me, just this once. Please . . .' I pouted. 'Pretty please.'

'No!' he said. But he couldn't help smiling. 'Put your lip back in, I'm not going to fall for it this time.'

I pictured Jack tripping over a giant lip and chuckled to myself. 'You know what?' I said. 'You could be a maths teacher – you're so good at explaining this stuff.' My imagination must have been in overdrive that evening because then a picture of Jack in a horrible jacket, with cord trousers and greasy hair came into my mind, which wasn't what I'd intended at all. I flicked it away. 'In a good way, I mean. A cool maths teacher.'

'I don't want to be a maths teacher,' he said, frowning.

I already knew that; Jack wants to be a sports reporter. 'Yeah, but you'd be good at it. Better than Mr Reynolds. And much, much fitter.'

He reddened. 'Anyone would be better than Mr Reynolds. Come on, we've got five more questions to get through and then we can chill.'

I ignored him. 'The girls would love you. You'd be the most popular teacher ever. You'd have them queuing in the corridor.'

He laughed and tapped my exercise book with his pen, just like Mr Reynolds does. 'Stop trying to flatter me, it won't work. Come on, let's do the next question.'

I pretended to sulk. If I wanted to talk about Alex, I was going to have to risk coming straight out with it.

'Did you help Alex with her maths homework too?' I asked, quietly. I was really nervous of his reaction. I hadn't dared bring up her name to Jack for weeks.

He hesitated. 'No.' He didn't sound annoyed, just surprised. 'She was better at maths than me,' he added. 'She didn't need my help.'

'Did you do your homework together?'

'Sometimes,' he said. 'We revised for our GCSEs together.'

I pictured Jack sitting with his arm around the smiling girl I'd seen on Topfriendz and felt a shard of jealousy slice into me. Was there anything Jack and I had done together that he hadn't already done with Alex? Was there anything she wasn't better at than me?

'So was she a total swot?' I asked. I wanted him to put her down, to say she was boring.

'No,' he said, a bit too defensively. 'She was just naturally good at it. It was one of her A-level options. Last thing I knew, she was planning to do it at university.'

'Oh, I see,' I said, feeling a little hiccup of guilt. Jack was wrong. I knew Alex had dropped maths at the beginning of Sixth Form, because she'd told me.

'You really liked her, didn't you, Jack? Do you think about her a lot?'

'Not really,' he said. He sounded impatient now. 'Do you think about your exes?'

I wanted to answer, 'I don't really have any, not proper ones, anyway, not serious ones,' but Jack's question was rhetorical. 'Actually,' he continued, 'don't answer that. I don't want to know. How did we get on to this, anyway?'

I knew that was that: he'd slammed the door shut on our conversation about Alex. Same old, same old. Jack wasn't going to tell me what had gone wrong between them, or why she had finished the relationship. And maybe he never would. Either he didn't want me to know, or it was so awful he couldn't bring himself to talk about it.

'Sorry, Jack.'

'It's OK, it's just not that important. It's the past and now I'm with you.' He closed my maths textbook and moved closer towards me, putting his arm across my shoulders.

'Don't,' I said. 'The door's open and my parents are downstairs.'

'Let's go outside to my car, then.'

I nodded.

'I'm just going out to say goodbye to Jack,' I shouted, as we walked down the stairs, arm in arm.

Dad came into the hall. 'You've got five minutes!' he said, firmly. 'After that, I'm coming out to find you.'

Dad hated the fact that Jack had a car. If he wasn't worrying that he would speed and crash, mangling us both, he'd worried that we'd get up to no good in a car park.

'God, my dad is so uptight,' I said, as we clambered into the car. It's not true – my dad is a pussycat – but it gave me an easy path on to the subject of dads and I figured this might be my very last opportunity to uncover some information. 'Was your dad strict too, Jack?'

He stiffened and moved away a fraction.

'Yes,' he said. He wasn't looking at me.

'Did he ground you and stuff? Were you allowed out on weeknights?'

'It wasn't like that.' He took his arm away from my shoulders and I was suddenly aware how cold it was in the car. 'What is up with you tonight, Lily? I feel like I'm in Guantanemo Bay, being interrogated. I've told you before, I don't want to talk about him.'

'Why not?'

'I just don't.'

'You can trust me, you know,' I said, softly. As soon as I said it, I had the horrible realisation that it wasn't true.

'Yes, I know. But it's in the past and it's got nothing to do with anything. Just drop it, Lil, OK?'

'Sorry,' I said, again. Not sorry I asked, just sorry I'd upset him.

We sat in silence for a couple of minutes. Maybe I'd gone about it the wrong way. Maybe I always did. Did I keep asking the wrong questions, or make it too obvious that I was prying? Or was I just stupid? What had I expected, that he'd come round after college and suddenly confess his past to me, like a villain in a crime drama when they've been caught out by 'zee' clever detective? 'It's a fair cop, Lily, you've got me and now I'm going to tell you why that pesky Alex dumped me, and reveal the terrible truth about my tragically dead dad.' As if.

'You know, if you ever need to talk about it I'm here for you,' I said. And I really did mean that. I took his hand and he let me. 'I don't want you to be sad.'

'I'm not sad,' he said, unconvincingly. 'And one day I'll probably tell you about him. But I don't want to talk about it now. So don't ask me.'

'OK, Jack.' I tried hard not to sound too disappointed. There was another silence. 'Look, I should go back inside.'

He draped his arm over my shoulders again, drawing me towards him. 'We've only been out here for a few minutes,' he said. 'And it's freezing.'

I gave him a quick kiss on the lips and pulled away. 'I'm tired, Jack. Thanks for coming round though, it was really nice of you.'

'I know,' he said, with a wink. 'I am nice. Very nice.'

He stroked my hair, tucking it behind my ears for me. I loved it when he did that; nobody else ever has. It made me feel warm and tingly and special. I wanted to melt and let Jack kiss me, I really did, but I couldn't relax because I knew that very soon I'd have to go back inside and email Alex to say I was coming to the match.

'My dad will be out in a second,' I said, pulling away. He looked confused. 'Good night, Jack.' And before he could try to stop me, I opened the door, climbed out of the car and ran into my house.

I thought about Jack a lot as I waited for Alex to arrive at the football stadium. I thought how I'd rather be with him than here, sprawling across the sofa, ruffling his hair. I remembered how disappointed he was when I told him I had to see Katie that afternoon, and how the anxious look that rippled across his face for just an instant revealed that he wondered if I might be going off him. He didn't say anything, but I could tell he was thinking it wasn't like me to rush off or to cancel an arrangement. He was right. It isn't like me. Or at least, it didn't used to be. Perhaps it was like Laura.

I also thought about how many times I'd had to lie that day, and to how many people. White lies and black lies. Huge lies and tiny ones.

There was the biggest lie of all, the megawatt lie: I'd lied to Jack. Not only by what I'd said, but by what I hadn't said.

I'd lied to Alex, over and over, and I was about to spend an afternoon telling her still more lies.

I'd lied to my parents, who would never have allowed

me to go to a football match with a strange girl and her dad, let alone travel there by myself.

And, if I'm keeping count, I was also about to lie to Alex's dad.

All that lying made me feel empty. Empty and a little bit sad. Perhaps, I thought, I should have called myself Liar Thompson, not Laura Thompson. Laura the liar. Liar Laura. Lira. Interesting how it was almost the same word. Was it an accident that I'd chosen that name . . .?

'Laura!'

There was a hand resting lightly on my shoulder. I'd been so immersed in my thoughts I hadn't heard anyone approaching. I jumped out of my skin. Into Laura's.

'I knew it was you,' said Alex. She was taller than me, slender and healthy-looking, without a jot of make-up on her face. 'I've been calling you. Didn't you hear?'

Of course I hadn't heard. I wasn't programmed to answer to someone else's name. My heart was beating so fast it was hard to speak without gasping. I willed it to slow down. 'No, sorry. I was in a dream.'

'Anyhow. Hello, Laura,' she said, beaming a big-toothed smile. She leaned over to give me a hug. 'It's so great to finally see you again.'

'Hello Alex, I'm Laura,' I said, slowly and deliberately, as if by repeating the name I might make it stick. 'It's good to see you too.'

# Chapter 10

♡

Nobody would have recognised me. At least, I hope not, because that was my intention. On the morning of the match I'd woken early and asked myself, 'What would Laura wear?', the answer to which was an emphatic, 'Nothing you've got in your wardrobe!' No doubt, worrying about Laura's outfit was a way of distracting myself from the nerve-wracking task ahead. I felt as if I was about to perform in a play without having seen the script. It would help if at least the costume were right.

Katie had saved the day (or so I thought) when she came to 'pick me up for shopping' by bringing me a pair of black jogging bottoms, a stripy black and white T-shirt with buttons at the collar, which had once belonged to her older brother, and her black quilted zip-up jacket. This was the closest to 'sporty' that either of us could get. To complete the look, I'd tied my hair into a high ponytail with a pink scrunchie, a bit like I had it in Laura's profile picture on Topfriendz. I studied myself in the mirror, and a girl with no dress sense stared back at me. Lily, meet Laura.

'What do you think?' I asked Katie. 'Will Laura do for a football match?'

'You look hideous,' she said. 'It's perfect.'

'I look like Vicky Pollard after she's been run over on a zebra crossing. And that's supposed to be good? Alex has taste, remember. She went out with Jack.'

'Not that much taste – she dumped him, *remember*?'

'Fair point. The only good thing is I feel less nervous now I'm done up as Laura. It's like when we went to that fancy dress party and I could act totally stupid because I didn't feel like me.'

'Probably best not to bring that up,' said Katie, wincing. 'I'm still trying to erase it from my memory.'

Alex didn't seem all that impressed with my sartorial efforts. One of the first things she said to me, as we walked up the stairs towards the stand entrance with her dad, was, 'Are you sure you support Arsenal?'

I felt a jolt of fear. Had I been discovered? 'What do you mean?'

Her eyes scrolled down my body. 'Your clothes. I'm worried they won't let you in.'

I wasn't sure whether to feel relieved or insulted. I

glanced at Alex's outfit. She had on a pair of faded jeans, with a white T-shirt and a red hoodie – the type of clothes I'd normally wear. Around her neck was a red and white woolly scarf. 'What's wrong? Do I look too chavvy?'

'God, no. I didn't mean that at all, I wasn't being rude. It's the colours. Had you forgotten, we're playing Newcastle today. You're wearing black and white stripes – their colours.' She pointed to a sign above the entrance. It read: *No away colours permitted.* 'You'll have to sit with the away fans, if you're not careful.' She giggled.

'Oh God,' I said, trying to think on my feet. In all my anxiety about meeting Alex, I hadn't remembered to look up the details of the match on the web. 'Silly me. I thought that was next week's fixture. I was in such a hurry this morning, I just didn't think.'

'Never mind,' she said, smiling reassuringly. 'Have you got any cash? We need to buy you a scarf.'

I looked in my purse; I had ten pounds, enough to buy some coffees and for my fare home. 'This is all I've got,' I said, holding it out to her. 'Is that enough?'

'Don't worry, my dad will lend you some, won't you, Dad?'

Alex's dad smiled at me. He was also tall and slim, with a full head of silver-grey hair, and the same toothy grin as his daughter. 'That's fine,' he said, taking a twenty-pound note out of his wallet and passing it to me. 'No need to pay me back.'

'No, no, I can't take your money,' I said, waving his

hand away. I meant it. I felt bad enough about deceiving Alex, but her dad, who seemed really sweet, was totally innocent in all this. Taking his money was like extortion; I could probably get arrested for it. *Con Woman Arrested at Football Match* the headline would read. *A teenage con woman stole the life savings from a kindly old man . . .*

'I insist,' he said, pressing the note into my hand and closing my fist around it. 'It's nice to finally meet a friend of Alex's who shares her passion for football.'

'Thank you,' I muttered. I couldn't look him in the eye.

Alex took me into the shop, while her dad waited outside. There were about five different scarf designs, which I could barely tell apart. 'You should get this one,' Alex said, pointing to a red and white striped scarf identical to hers. 'It's the latest one for this season.'

'Cool,' I said. 'It's great.' I paid for the scarf and then wound it around my shoulders, tying it at my neck. It felt scratchy and I could sense red, itchy welts forming on my skin underneath. In a strange way, I liked the discomfort; it would serve as a reminder that I couldn't let my guard down, that I must not relax and slip out of character.

'That's more like it,' said Alex's dad, with a warm smile, when he saw me. He wouldn't take the change. 'Buy me a cup of tea at half time.'

The stadium was enormous, with countless bars and restaurants surrounding a giant, perfectly manicured football pitch. It was strange to be in a place where there were so many more men than women. The background noise was a low rumble of deep voices and there was an overwhelming smell of clashing aftershaves mixed with beer. I was struck by the fact that there was no queue at all for the ladies' toilet, while the queue for the gents' snaked around the corner. It felt like a little victory. Hah! I thought. Finally they understand what it's like to be a girl.

As we walked outside to our seats – posh seats, because Alex's dad had got the tickets through work – I'll admit that even I was excited by the charged atmosphere, by the raucous singing and the sense of anticipation. All around me was a red and white sea of thousands of supporters wearing Arsenal strips and scarves. In one corner, the sea was broken up by a little puddle of black and white, the loyal away supporters who were doing their best to be heard over the din, trading insults with the home fans surrounding them. I zipped my jacket right up to my neck, so nobody could think I might be one them.

'When the camera comes round, smile and wave,' said Alex, as we sat down.

I tried not to show my panic. Camera, what camera? Jack was sure to be watching the match. I couldn't imagine anything worse than being seen on film, sitting right next to Alex. Talk about being caught red (or should that be red and white) handed. Even I wouldn't have been able to explain my way out of that one. '*What? Someone who looks like me was sitting next to your ex-girlfriend? At a football match, while I was out shopping with Katie? What are the chances of that?'*

'I don't want to be on telly,' I said, shuffling uncomfortably, even though my red plastic seat wasn't as hard as I'd expected.

'You're not shy, are you Laura?' She smiled at me. 'Don't worry, it's just for the fans in the stadium. The camera pans round and the pictures show up on those big screens.' She pointed to the corners of the ground, where there were giant screens showing the crowd. 'Of course there are TV cameras here too, but they usually focus on the super fans, the people with painted faces or big banners.'

'Oh,' I said. I still wasn't comfortable with the idea of being filmed. It wasn't worth the risk. What if one of Jack's friends was there? Or someone I knew, who might tell my parents they'd seen me?

Too late . . . 'Here we go . . . Wave!' said Alex, as the image on the screen showed the people directly to our left. I had a split second to think and so I did the only thing I could do – I kicked over the can of Coke that I'd placed at my feet, sending a stream of fizzy brown liquid over our shoes and bags.

'Whoops!' I cried, as I bent down to pick up the can, ensuring that the only image that might have appeared on screen was of the back of my head. As far as I know, the back of my head isn't particularly distinctive.

'Are you all right, Laura?'

'Yes. What a klutz I am,' I said. 'I'm really sorry about your bag and shoes. I'm so clumsy, I'm always doing stuff like that.' I made a mental note: remember, Laura is clumsy, it could come in handy,

'It's OK,' said Alex, wiping down her bag with a tissue she'd found in her pocket. 'You made us miss our moment of glory, though.'

I shrugged. 'Sorry.'

'Forget it. Hey, we're about to kick off. Excellent, we won the toss.'

As the match got underway, I soon realised that, in spite of my enforced football studies, I still had a lot to learn about the game and, more specifically, the individual players. Without the benefit of a television zoom lens, or any commentary, I found it hard to tell one player from another. They were all dressed the same, after all.

'Isn't Walcott playing well today?' said Alex.

'Oh yes.'

'Do you think he's better off in this position?'

'Sure,' I said. 'It suits him.' Just agree with whatever she says, I thought.

'Who's your favourite player, Laura?'

'Um . . .' I wracked my brain. Who did Jack say he liked again? 'Thierry Henry.'

'Yeah, he's everyone's favourite. But he's left. I mean current players.'

Try to remember, Lily. Who did Jack talk about last

week? 'I think Rosicky is playing really well,' I said. 'And he's cute, too.'

'I agree with you there, Laura. But he's on the bench.'

Shit. 'Really? Are you sure? I'm positive I saw him at the other end.' I thought quickly. 'It's because I don't have my glasses on. I feel like a right idiot. I didn't bring them because they make me really self-conscious and I was meeting up with you for the first time, and you know . . .'

'Don't worry about it,' said Alex. 'I wear contacts. If I didn't have them in I wouldn't be able to tell if I was watching football or tennis.'

I know the feeling.

The other details of the match don't bear repeating, except to say that Arsenal won by two goals to nil and that, yes, footballers' legs are even nicer in the flesh, especially when you're deliberately squinting a lot. Fearful of tripping myself up again, I said as little as I could to Alex, which was fine because she was so enthralled by the game. I clapped when she clapped, cheered when she cheered and groaned with her too. She kept glancing over and smiling at me, in a way which said she was glad we were sharing this experience, that it was bonding us. I smiled back, guiltily. Maybe there's something to be said for pretending to enjoy yourself, though, because I have to admit the match really wasn't all that bad and the hour and a half passed very quickly. Oh, and I didn't buy Alex's dad a cup of tea at half time because it turned out the tea was free. When we got to the front of the queue and he saw the realisation dawn on me, he winked.

His car was parked about a ten-minute walk from the ground. It smelled new and leathery, not like my parents' car, which always smells of nappies and baby lotion. My brother Eric, also known as 'the accident' (by my parents) and 'the pain' (by me), still wears them, even though he's nearly three.

'I'll drop you off at the coffee place on the high street and come back for you in a couple of hours,' said Alex's dad.

'Cheers,' said Alex. 'Are you still up for coffee, Laura?'

I nodded, vigorously. Of course I was. Sod the football, the talking part was the whole point of the day for me.

Alex's dad parked up and got out of the car to say goodbye. He came round to my side, opened my door for me and offered his hand to help me out. 'Thank you, Laura, for the pleasure of your company. You're welcome to join us again any time you want.'

'Thank you,' I said, reddening with guilt. Why did he have to be so sweet? 'And thanks again for the ticket.' I felt horrible, like I'd just trodden in something nasty and was walking it through his home.

I bought the coffees; it was the least I could do. Alex had a skinny cappuccino and I had a mocha, with extra chocolate on top, because I don't really like the taste of coffee but I didn't want to say so. I think the way you drink coffee says just as much about you as the way you eat pizza, and I'm not talking about reading coffee grounds or any of that airy-fairy rubbish. You can tackle the froth delicately with a spoon, as if it's a dessert (my preferred method), or you can pick up the cup and drink it straight down, risking what's known as a Belgian dip (when you get froth all over your nose). Alex did neither. She sipped her coffee so slowly from the side of the cup that the froth barely moved at all, and was left coating the bottom when she'd finished. If I hadn't already known how different we were, I knew it then.

'So, I've been dying to ask you this all afternoon,' she said. 'Do you think I've changed a lot since camp? I hardly recognised you.'

How could I answer that? 'Massively,' I lied, although it was perfectly true to say I hadn't recognised her, because it really was the very first time I'd seen her. 'I mean you look so different.' I paused and then embellished my lie with flattery. 'You're much prettier now.'

'Thanks, Laura. So are you. I guess we've both grown up and changed a lot.'

'Yes, it's a long time ago. A whole world away.'

I didn't want to dwell on this subject, it was too uncomfortable. 'You were telling me about the holiday you'd planned for the summer,' I said, sounding like a hairdresser making smalltalk. 'Tell me more . . .'

We chatted for a while about nothing in particular – music we'd bought, books we'd read, films we'd been to see. Alex laughed a lot; she seemed to find me, or Laura, very amusing. It felt much like being with any new friend in a café, the only difference being that this one kept calling me Laura. I imagined that this was what it must be like to be in a witness protection programme, with a new identity and a new history (if you ignore the fact that I was still in the process of committing the crime). It surprised me how quickly I was starting to get used to my new name, how it was beginning to feel like it belonged to me, the way a new nickname does when people use it often enough. It wasn't just the name: I was starting to inhabit Laura too. In just one day, she had fleshed out considerably. She wasn't just a user name on the internet any more, or the label at the top of a message; she had individual characteristics which were distinct from mine, and most of which had been acquired by accident. She dressed differently from me, was clumsy and short-sighted and she even spoke more slowly and precisely, mainly because I had to think so carefully about every word she said. If I lived as Laura for a few weeks or a few months, I wondered, would I actually become her? Was I being myself when I talked to Alex, or Laura? Or was I a mix of the two? Had inventing Laura changed me?

My thoughts were interrupted by a loud bleeping from my phone. Why hadn't I remembered to put it on silent?

'You've got a text,' said Alex, who either thought I was a bit deaf or just liked stating the obvious. I fumbled my bag and pulled out the badly behaved device, making sure that Alex couldn't see the screen. Horror of horrors, it was a message from Jack.

*U still wth KT? Cnt w8 2 c u 2nite. xxxx*

Should I ignore it? Or would that make it more obvious that I had something to hide?

'Ah, it's from Jared,' I said. 'He wants to know if I enjoyed the match. And he says hi to you.' God, I was getting good. Or should that be evil?

'Tell him hi back,' she said. 'I'd love to meet him some time.'

Over my dead body, I thought. 'Definitely,' I said. 'We'll have to arrange it. Do you mind if I just text him back?'

She shook her head.

I quickly texted. *Y. Me 2. Cll u l8tr xxxx* And then, pretending that I was still labouring over my message, I modified my address book so that 'Jack' became simply 'J'.

J for Jack. J for Jared. And, it now strikes me, J for Judas.

'Hey,' said Alex, as I started to turn my phone off. 'I've just twigged: we don't have each other's numbers. Now that we've met it would be nice to be able to talk to you, as well as message each other.'

'That's right, we don't,' I said, as if I was surprised. It hadn't been an oversight; I deliberately hadn't asked Alex for her number or offered her mine. My reason was simple: what if Alex rang or texted me while I was with Jack?

'Here, take mine,' she said.

I couldn't say no. Thinking quickly, I opened a new entry in my address book and typed in *Jared*. That way, there would be no trace of Alex's name on my phone. The name would also serve as an alert: either to switch off my phone altogether, or, if I was alone, to become Laura. When, later, I told Katie what I'd done, she codenamed my mission to find out Jack's secrets 'Project Jared'.

'Ready?' said Alex. 'It's 079 . . .'

I'm not going to repeat her whole number; it's private. I don't need anything else to feel guilty about.

'Thanks,' I said, and gave her mine. I'll admit I did think, briefly, about changing one of the digits. I thought better of it: it would have been futile, no more than a delaying tactic, and would merely have aroused her suspicions.

It was time to be brave, time to get to the point. 'So,' I ventured, 'I've told you all about Jared, but you never really talk about your love life. I know you're single at the moment, but is there anyone you like?'

'Not really,' she said. 'There's this guy at college who's quite buff, but he's really just a friend. We almost snogged once, but that's all. I don't really want to get into anything serious with anyone.'

'Why's that?' I asked, fishing, hopeful that she would bring up Jack.

She didn't. 'You know, going away to uni next year and all. Seems stupid to.'

'Oh right,' I said. I changed tack. 'Have you been single for a long time?'

'About a year. I had a long-term boyfriend before that, but it didn't work out.'

Finally! I tried not to show the excitement that was rising in my chest. 'What was he like?' I asked, just to be certain that she was talking about Jack, just to be one hundred per cent sure that I wasn't sitting in a coffee shop, in disguise, with the wrong Alex Porter. You can't be too careful. It's not as if I had sampled her DNA, had I?

'He was lovely,' she said, her eyes growing sad. 'Kind, cute, funny. Pretty much perfect. He was my first proper boyfriend and I was his first serious girlfriend. We got together when we were fourteen.' She sighed. 'I can't believe I'm telling you all this, the first time we've met. You're really easy to talk to, Laura, a really good listener. Anyway, a lot of stuff happened. Maybe we were just too young for it to last.'

Her obvious sadness confused me. Did she regret breaking up with him? 'He sounds amazing,' I said. 'But if he was so perfect, why did you finish with him?'

She looked at me, strangely. 'I didn't,' she said. 'I don't know where you got that idea. He broke up with me. He broke my heart.' Her eyes appeared moist, as if she was on the brink of tears. She got up from the table. 'I'm going to get another coffee. Same again?'

# Chapter 11

♡

Why would Jack say he'd been dumped by Alex, when he hadn't? Why, for that matter, would anyone claim to be the 'dumpee', when they were actually the dumper? What possible reason could there be? It's not exactly something you brag about, is it? In my experience, if someone doesn't want you to know that their girlfriend or boyfriend had enough of them, they say, 'The break-up was mutual,' which we all know is code for 'I was dumped, I'm gutted, but I'm not going to admit it.' But Jack had always been very clear: Alex had finished with him. *She* was the one who'd ended the relationship, for reasons which were far too painful to talk about. So, if it clearly wasn't about protecting his pride, what was it about? Gaining my sympathy? No, because if that were the case, Jack would have furnished his story with details, instead of shutting me out. Had he cheated on her, or done something else to hurt her, something he was too ashamed to admit? Maybe he'd told Alex their relationship was over before she found out what he'd done, to save her feelings and his reputation. It was the only possibility that made any kind of sense. And yet, that didn't seem to ring true either.

I wondered about this long after I'd said goodbye to Alex, all the way home from the coffee shop and in my bedroom, as I got ready to see Jack. So much for uncovering the information I'd been after; I had come away from my afternoon with Alex with far more questions than answers, more doubts than certainties.

'Hello, Laura Thompson,' said Katie, after I'd texted her to say it was safe to call.

'Very funny,' I said. 'Did you get a nice dress on your shopping trip with your best mate?'

'Oh yes, it's skintight leopard print, with sequins and a bow,' she deadpanned. 'And frills. Want to borrow it? Or are trackie bottoms more your style now?'

'Ha. Ha. Ha. Actually, I've just de-Laura-ed myself. I can't tell you how good it feels to be back in my own clothes and, literally, to let my hair down. Honestly, if I wore my hair up that tight all the time I'd end up with a receding hairline.'

'And a facelift,' said Katie. 'Go on then, tell me all about it . . .'

I told Katie everything: about my potential wardrobe

malfunction, about how sweet Alex's dad was, and how I'd surprised myself by not entirely hating the match.

'Really?' she asked. 'Are you sure? Can I take your temperature?'

I told her what Alex had said about Jack and how it didn't make any sense, and she seemed just as puzzled as me. She asked what I was planning to do about it and I said there was only one thing I could do: to keep in touch with Alex and hope that she spilled. And soon. Now that Alex had my phone number, deleting her from my life wouldn't be as straightforward as I'd planned. I'd have to keep the façade going for as long as it took. I'd probably have to see her again. Katie seemed a bit put out by this. In fact, a few times during our conversation, she tried to belittle Alex.

'So was she really boring then, a total sports nerd?' she asked.

'No,' I said. 'She was different from us, but I really liked her. It wasn't hard to talk to her.'

'You don't seriously think you could be mates, do you?'

'I don't know. Maybe.'

'Listen to yourself, Lily. She is not your friend. She can't ever be your friend. Apart from the fact you don't have anything real in common with her – if you don't count Jack, anyway – you're a lying, cheating impostor. And when she finds out she's going to hate you.'

'God, you don't have to be so cold about it,' I said. I was upset, even though I knew what she'd said was true.

'I'm just giving you a reality check,' said Katie. 'I think you're getting in too deep. I think maybe you're even enjoying the lying part a little bit, and that's twisted.'

'And I think you're just jealous.'

'Yeah, right,' she said. 'Jealous of a tomboy who doesn't even know your real name and has to make friends over the internet. I don't think so.'

We were both silent for a few minutes, which is very awkward (not to mention a waste of credit) when you're on the phone. You can hear the other person breathing and swallowing, and any background noise around them. Soon, you start to feel silly but you don't want to be the first person to speak, to give in. So you sulk until someone cracks.

I think, on this occasion, that it was me who spoke first. I said sorry and then we made up and everything was cool. All best mates bicker, don't they? Katie and I don't argue very often – I can't remember the last fight before that day – but I'm sure I've read somewhere that it's healthy to have the odd falling out. It shows you care and that you have your own personality, or something like that.

Jack was due round at eight, which didn't leave me much time to get my head together. One of the advantages of having a little brother is that you can spend Saturday night in alone with your boyfriend. It's a trade-off: you give up your plans and babysit for free, so your parents can go out, and they reward you with the company of your oh-so-trustworthy boyfriend, who you'd otherwise be seeing. There's no way in hell my parents would ever have let us stay in alone together if Eric hadn't been asleep upstairs but, somehow, him being there made it all right. What did they think, that he'd start crying on cue if things got a bit frisky on the sofa? Maybe they imagined the sight of a screaming toddler would act as a deterrent – a reminder of what the consequences of misbehaving could be.

Although I was looking forward to seeing Jack, part of me wished he'd call and cancel, so I could have some space to think things through and to calm down. I was troubled by what Alex had told me and needed time to process it before seeing him. I was also physically exhausted, drained by having so much adrenalin surging through my veins for all those hours. All I really wanted was a night in with a hot chocolate and a magazine. Jack was bound to notice if I was quiet and he would ask what was wrong, and I'd have to make up yet another lie. I still hadn't got my story straight about 'my afternoon with Katie'. He would ask about that too, even though he wasn't remotely interested in Katie's choice of dress. Sometimes I wished he wasn't so darned considerate.

I glanced in the mirror and the same features, arranged in the usual order, glanced back at me. But I felt unsettled. Everything looked the same and yet something was different. Even though I'd taken off Laura's clothes, untied her hair and tried to wash the remnants of her away in the bath, a tiny part of her was clinging on to me, like a ghost hovering in the shadows.

'Lily,' Mum called. 'Jack's just pulling up outside. Eric's fast asleep. Come and say goodbye.'

I took a deep breath. Weird how suddenly my own name didn't sound entirely familiar. 'Coming . . .'

Jack looked so handsome when he came in that I almost forgot all my worries. He leaned down to kiss me hello and he smelled gorgeous, like soap and fresh towels. When I placed my hand on the nape of his neck I could feel that his hair was still damp from the shower. We stood in the hall kissing for a few minutes, before I took his hand and led him through to the living room.

'Can I get you a drink?' I asked, as we sat down. 'We've got the usual: Coke, Ribena, orange juice. Oh, and Mum bought some gross ginger cordial.'

'Sure,' he said. 'Whatever you're having.'

When I came back into the room, he was grinning at me.

'What's that?' he asked, motioning to my bag, which was lying by the side of the sofa where I'd dumped it. I almost dropped the drinks in horror. Spilling out from one corner was a length of tasselled red and white wool, the end of my Arsenal scarf, which I'd stuffed inside it on the journey home. I'd intended to take my bag upstairs and hide the scarf in my wardrobe, but something had distracted me and I'd forgotten. How could I have been so careless?

'It's a handbag,' I said, dryly, hoping against hope that

93

he hadn't noticed. I put the drinks down on the coffee table, my hands shaking. 'Girls use them to put things in.'

'Oh you should be on at the Comedy Store with your wit. I mean that – the red and white stripy thing that's hanging out of it. Is that what I think it is?'

'That depends what you think it is.'

'Don't tease me, Lil. It looks like an official Arsenal scarf, the latest design. How come you've got a brand new Arsenal scarf in your bag?'

That was a *very* good question.

I breathed deeply. 'It's a present,' I said. Lying was beginning to come as naturally to me as blinking. 'For you. It was supposed to be a surprise. I was going to wrap it up for you and give it to you another time.'

'You don't need to do that.' He opened his eyes very wide. 'Can I have it now?'

'Hang on,' I said. 'I just need to take the price label off. Stay there. I'll be back in a second.'

I picked up the bag and took it through into the kitchen, so that I could do a quick examination of the scarf. I needed to make sure there weren't any visible clues that could reveal it wasn't the gift I claimed it to be. I was relieved to see there were no tea stains or bobbling, but it did smell strongly of my perfume. I'll have to make that a feature, I thought. I rummaged in my bag for my perfume spray and gave the scarf three quick spritzes. Then I folded it neatly, so that it looked as good as new again. 'I'm coming back in now,' I called. 'Close your eyes.'

Jack was sitting on the sofa with a big grin on his face, his eyes shut tight and his hands cupped. He appeared like an excited little boy, barely older than Eric. It made me feel doubly bad about my deceit and, just for a millisecond, I wanted to confess everything.

'Can I open them yet?'

'Be patient.' I swept the scarf across Jack's face, brushing his cheeks with the tassels. He ducked and tried to grab the scarf from my hands, pulling me off balance and on to his lap. I tickled him until he let me go. 'I want to put it on you,' I said, clambering up and wrapping the scarf around his head, mummy-style, so that his eyes and nose peeped through. 'That's perfect.'

He stood up and looked in the mirror behind the sofa, the one I can never see because I'm not tall enough. 'Wow!' he said, as he unravelled the scarf from his face and draped it around his neck. 'Mmm, it smells of you too. That's fantastic, Lil, thanks so much. It's so thoughtful. I think it's probably the nicest thing anyone's ever given me. I've been wanting one of these for ages. When did you get it? Did you go all the way to the ground?'

'I got it today,' I said, wondering how Mr Porter would feel if he knew he'd inadvertently bought a gift for the guy who had broken his daughter's heart. 'Katie and I didn't really go shopping for a dress, this afternoon . . .' I backtracked, realising I'd already described Katie's 'wicked new dress' to my parents. It was best not to contradict myself. 'Well, we did, but we also went to the Arsenal shop.'

'Thanks so much,' he said, beaming. He lifted me on to his back so that I could see in the mirror too and then he carefully turned me around and kissed me until my jaw ached.

Can a lie that makes someone that happy really be a bad thing?

Eric did a good job of ruining our evening together, waking up several times with bad dreams and refusing to go back to sleep until we read him a story. And then read it to him again. Jack was much more patient with him than I was; he always was. Maybe it was because he didn't have a dad and so he'd had to take on that role with his younger sister. I had a suspicion that Eric liked Jack more than he likes me. Little kids can tell if you're just going through the motions with them.

'So what do you fancy watching?' I asked Jack, when we'd finally got Eric to settle. 'I've got a couple of DVDs that I know you'd like. Or we could just listen to some music.'

Jack widened his eyes. How did he make them twinkle like that, on cue? 'Well . . . *Match of the Day* is on soon, you know. And I happen to know the Arsenal game is on first.'

I froze. Not the match, anything but the match. I thought I'd got away with it. Jack clearly hadn't spotted me in the crowd when he'd watched the game live that afternoon, but people always notice fresh details the second time around. What if there were different shots, taken from different angles? 'Oh Jack, do we have to? I whined. 'I mean, you know I like football now and all, but I'm not in the mood. Haven't you already seen it once today?'

'Yeah, but my mum kept calling me out to help her carry stuff, so I missed quite a lot. I'd just like to see the goals again. And anyway, it gives me an excuse to wear my new scarf. Hey, we can pretend we're on the terraces together, watching it for real.'

It wasn't much of an imaginative leap for me.

'Oh goody,' I said, sarcastically. 'I hope you've brought your rattle.'

'Please Lil, just this once, let me . . .'

I couldn't think of a good enough excuse to refuse him. 'Oh go on,' I said, handing him the remote control. I probably shouldn't admit this, but there was something a tiny bit thrilling about the risk I was taking. Would I be able to see myself? Would it be as I'd remembered?

He kissed me. 'Thanks, Lily. Have I ever told you that you're the best girlfriend in the world?'

'No I'm not,' I said, quietly. I don't think he noticed my change in tone.

I was lucky; very little of the match was shown and the crowd shots were sparse. If I couldn't spot myself, I'm certain nobody else could either. The hardest thing was pretending not to know what happened next so I could react with the correct emotion – surprise, awe or anger – when all I felt was familiarity. But it's always better to be safe than sorry, and so, whenever I thought the camera was panning around to the part of the stadium in which Alex and I had been sitting, I'd simply move in for a snog. If Jack tried to resist, I'd poke him in his side and make him squirm with laughter.

'God, you're affectionate tonight,' said Jack, when I allowed him to come up for air. 'I missed that goal again! Not that I'm complaining or anything. It's good.' He hesitated. 'Really good. You've been so distant lately that I thought you were going to finish with me.'

Like Alex *finished* with you, I thought. It was still niggling me, however hard I tried to push it to the back of my mind. 'No, don't be silly. Of course not. I've just been tired and stressed with schoolwork, you know.'

'Course,' he said, as usual accepting what I said at face value. 'As if you could get sick of this mug.' He gurned at me.

I grabbed hold of both his cheeks and squeezed them hard. 'Congratulations Jack. You're still in the running to becoming Britain's Next Top Gargoyle.'

He smiled, switched off the television and gently took my hands, then looked at me with real intensity, as if he was trying to decipher my thoughts (and, let's face it, it's a very good thing that he couldn't). 'You know what, I was being serious,' he said. 'I really did think you were going off me. And it was a total bummer, because I realised I was beginning to fall for you in a big way, which I wasn't expecting to happen.'

My mouth fell open. I didn't know what to say. Where was this coming from?

'I thought about it a lot, especially after the other night, and I figured that it was my fault if you were getting fed up with me. I know I probably haven't been as open with you as I should have been. It's hard sometimes, when you've been hurt before. I don't find it easy to open up to anyone. I've only ever done it once and, well, it didn't work out.'

I shook my head. 'I probably ask too many questions,' I said, ever the mistress of understatement. 'I can't help it. You know me, I'm not exactly Little Miss Patient.'

'You're fine,' he said. 'It's me. I've been too cagey. I needed to be sure of you before I told you. Now I think I am.'

'Told me what?' I asked. I was aware that he was still holding my hands and that my palms were hot and sweaty. I tried to let go, but he only clung on more tightly.

'I want to tell you about my dad,' he said. 'I think I should.'

I gasped and choked at the same time, swallowing so much air that I felt dizzy. Was this some sort of cosmic joke? On the same day that I'd crossed – more like pole-vaulted over – the line of no return by going to meet Alex, Jack had finally decided to open up to me. Thanks very much, Universe. You're good, I'll give you that.

'You don't have to,' I said. It was the polite thing to say, but I didn't mean it. No one ever does, do they?

'I want to.' He let go of my hands. 'But you've got to promise me you'll try to understand why I lied, and not hate me for it.'

I nodded. What did he mean, *he'd* lied? About what?

'I don't really know where to start,' he said. The sparkle in his eyes was gone; they looked steely grey. 'I'm just going to come straight out with it . . . Lily, my dad isn't dead.'

# chapter 12

♡

*Katie said her mum knew that her dad was having an affair because he kept buying her flowers and gifts. She called them guilt tokens. I think I understand why he did it. Giving Jack the scarf and seeing his reaction made me feel better about everything I'd done. It eased my conscience. So does that mean I'm like Katie's dad? Does it mean I was unfaithful to Jack? I don't think you could call what I did cheating; there was no other guy. You could call it enterprising. You could call it sneaky, even dodgy. But not unfaithful. I had Jack's best interests at heart all the way along. And what he didn't know couldn't hurt him, right?*

'My dad isn't dead,' Jack repeated. 'At least, not as far as I know. I mean, he might be. I haven't spoken to him for five years. But he didn't die when I was twelve.'

Jack stopped, as if to check whether I'd understood what he'd said. I think he'd expected some sort of reaction, something more vocal than me just sitting there with my mouth hanging open. But I was so stunned that I didn't have a clue what I could say.

'We left him then,' he continued, 'and we haven't seen him since. We don't want to, either.'

'It's OK,' I said, softly, finding my voice. 'What happened? You only have to tell me if you want to.'

'He wasn't a good dad, Lily, or a good man.' He laughed. 'That's way too kind. He was a piece of shit. He treated my mum like he owned her. He hurt her – physically, I mean. He used to beat her and kick her and throw things at her. It went on for years, from when I was little. Nobody outside had a clue what he was doing. He wasn't some drunken yob. He was a teacher, believe it or not: Mr Respectable. He was very clever about it. He'd never hit her in the face or anywhere it might show. There was this one time when he broke her rib and she could hardly breathe properly, and the next night they had to go to some school function, and she put on her lipstick and did her hair and went, like nothing was wrong. I really hated him for that.'

I thought of Jack's mum. I liked her. She seemed strong and in control, not the terrified, meek woman he was describing. 'Why didn't she leave him?' I asked.

'I don't know, why do people do anything? Why did he hit her? I think at first she still really loved him and hoped he'd stop. He promised he would; every time he did it he said he was sorry and it was the last time. Yeah, until the next time. Maybe she thought it was her fault. He said she deserved it because she was stupid and she got things wrong. Like using the wrong plates or putting too much pepper in the soup – if he was in *that* mood, it could be anything. Everyone else thought he was so wonderful, she probably thought it *was* her. She didn't think anyone would believe her if she told on him. He knew that; he told her people would laugh at her or think she was mad. And it probably had to do with money too: she was looking after me and Ruth and not working, and she didn't want us to lose our home and our friends.'

'Oh my God, Jack,' I said. I stroked his arm, uselessly, hoping it would be some comfort.

'There's more,' he said. 'When I got older, like nine or ten, and I was a bit taller and stronger, I'd try to protect Mum. I could tell when he was going to lose it – you pick up on these things after a while – and I'd get in between them so he couldn't hurt her. Sometimes it would work and he'd storm off, other times he'd just push me out of the way. And then, one day, when I'd just turned twelve, he went for me too. I was up in my room and I could hear him screaming at Mum, and Ruth was crying next door, and I just lost it. I'd had enough of him, you know?'

Breathlessly, he paused, looking to me for approval. I nodded.

'So I went downstairs and picked up the hammer from his tool box, which was out because he'd been putting up some shelves, I think. I wasn't planning to bash his brains in, or anything like that, although there were many times I could have done. It was just the first thing I found. I don't know what I was going to do with it, I think I was just going to threaten him with it so he'd leave Mum alone. Anyway, I went into the living room where they were and I held up the hammer and shouted, 'If you touch my mum again I'll hit you with this!' and he looked at me for a moment in shock, and I thought he was just going to walk out and . . .' His voice tailed off.

He appeared white, shrunken, as if he was twelve again and back in that room.

'It's OK,' I said. He didn't look at me, his eyes were downcast.

'So he's staring at me, like he can't believe what he's seeing, and then he laughs and he walked towards me, really calmly, and wrestles the hammer out of my hand. I crouch down, with my hands on my head, because I think he's going to go for me with it, but he drops it and instead gives me a really hard punch in the stomach. And I'm lying on the floor, I can't breathe properly – I'm winded, you know – and he starts on Mum and there's nothing I can do to help her. After that, it was like I'd unlocked something in him. A few days later, I said something he didn't like and he hit me again, on my arm this time, so it was black and blue for days. That's when Mum had enough. I can't remember how long it took – a couple of weeks, maybe, she must have been sorting things out – but that's when she took me and Ruth and we left Milton Keynes. Just got up one morning, packed our bags and left. So there you go, now you know about my dad.'

He looked up at me and the light seemed to swim back into his eyes. 'Do you see why I didn't tell you?'

'Yes,' I said. I smiled sympathetically, and hugged him. I was still unable to come up with any words that wouldn't sound trite or plain stupid. 'It's OK, Jack,' I said. 'It's OK.' But inside my head, I was talking ten to the dozen. No wonder Jack never let himself get wound up, I thought. No wonder he seemed older than his age. No wonder he hated fighting and would rather walk away and be called a chicken than be provoked. No wonder he did that martial art, which he explained was all about self-control and not lashing out. No wonder he'd got so weirdly upset when Eric was misbehaving and I threatened to smack him, even though I hadn't meant it. No wonder he seemed so perfect, because he'd made himself perfect, so nothing could get to him, and so he wasn't anything like his father.

'It's not something I like talking about,' he said, although now he'd started he seemed unable to stop. 'And for a while I couldn't talk about it because Mum was scared Dad would find us, so I didn't even tell anyone who I really was or where I'd really come from. There's something else I should tell you. My real name's not Jack Parmiter, that's an old family name from way back that Mum picked. I'm Jack Mullins, which probably sounds better, but it's *his* name, so he can keep it. We moved around a lot at first, I had to keep going to different schools, making new friends, starting all over again. It was really hard. The reason we came here was partly because of Mum's job and because we've got some family here in north London, but also because he tracked us down again and started making trouble. There's not a lot he can do now that I'm seventeen and Ruthie's fourteen. We don't have to see him any more, like we did at first. He just likes to make us all feel uncomfortable. He thinks we belong to him. He's like a stalker.'

Jack looked exhausted, but lighter somehow, as if he'd put down a heavy backpack that he'd been dragging around with him for months. 'So now you know everything,' he said. 'You're not saying anything, which isn't like you. Are you OK? What are you thinking?'

What was I thinking? I wasn't sure: all the thoughts in my head were jumbled up and knotted together. People say they collect their thoughts, as if they're collecting stamps, but for me it's always more like trying to sort a jar of hundreds and thousands into its constituent colours.

Jack had always seemed to me to be an equation which didn't make sense, like an x without a value. Now he added up. All my questions and frustrations had been justified; he *had* been hiding something from me, something which was an obstacle to getting to know him properly. What he'd told me wasn't what I'd been expecting – although I can't tell you exactly what I had expected. The truth wasn't glamorous or funny or outrageous, like the possibilities Katie and I had discussed, it was sad and grimy. If only he could have trusted me with it a little sooner, when I was still to be trusted.

I was also thinking how strong Jack was, and how brave, and how I was so much luckier than him because I'd never had to deal with anything really bad in my life. No one had ever hurt me, not really.

I was remembering all the times I'd moaned to Jack about my dad because he wouldn't let me stay out late or because he was a bit of a fusspot, and how he'd sympathised, when inside he must have been thinking I was blessed, and that made me cringe.

I was thinking how weird it was that I hadn't known Jack's real name and had simply accepted that he was called Parmiter, just as Alex hadn't thought to question whether I was christened Laura. The big difference was, of course, that Jack had changed his name to help keep him safe, while I'd changed mine because I was playing a game, because I was a nosy, impatient sneak.

And, most of all, I was thinking about confessing every last detail of what I'd done, so that absolutely everything was out in the open, so that there were no more lies and no more secrets. If there was a time for revelations, surely this was it.

In the end, what I said was: 'I'm just thinking how

amazing you are, Jack', and the moment, the opportunity to confess, was lost. It was a cop-out, I know, but I didn't have a clue where to start. Jack seemed so fragile and I couldn't bear to break him. He didn't need to know what I'd done. I'd find another way of making things right.

He held me, tightly. 'I'm surprised, but I'm actually really glad I told you,' he said.

'Me too,' I said.

He smiled. 'It's good that you know. I feel much closer to you now.'

'So do I,' I said, because I felt it was what he wanted to hear. And I wanted it to be true, I really did. But, if I'm honest, I felt more distant from Jack than ever before. Laura was no longer hovering in the corner of the room, she'd marched over and wedged herself right in between us.

# Chapter 13

♡

As soon as my parents had arrived home and Jack had left, I went into my bedroom, shut the door and texted Katie, asking her to call urgently. It was after eleven-thirty but I was sure she wouldn't be asleep. Not on a Saturday night. She'd mentioned something about going to the cinema with one of our friends, although, to be honest, I'd been so caught up in the dramas of my own day that I hadn't really listened.

There was a short delay and then my phone began to purr.

'What's up?' she slurred, drowsily, when I answered.

'You weren't asleep, were you?'

'Not really. Not any more,' she said, irritated. 'I told you, I decided not to go out tonight because I was feeling a bit dead. Has something happened? Does Jack know you went to the football?'

'No, it's not that.'

'Oh,' she said, in a voice which suggested I could have waited until the morning.

'Sorry I woke you. But it's all got so messy and complicated. I think I need to end things with Alex.'

'Oh,' she said again. 'So you want to terminate Project Jared, do you?'

'I'm being serious, Katie,' I said, and told her what had happened, repeating everything that Jack had told me. I'm not sure he meant for me to share the gruesome details about his father with anyone, but he hadn't actually said, 'Don't tell anyone', and he must realise that girls tell our best friends everything.

Katie listened, incredulous. When I'd finished, she said simply, 'Wow.'

'I know. I can't keep seeing Alex, can I? Not now Jack's opened up. I feel awful. Poor Jack. And what if he finds out what I've been doing? I'm not sure he'd understand.'

'Too right,' she said. 'But you weren't to know that Jack had some serious stuff going on in his past. You'd never have guessed what his dad did in a million years. He said he was dead, didn't he? So the way I see it, you haven't really done anything wrong. Jack lied to you, so you lied to him. You're even. But now you've got to stop it. You don't need Alex any more. You should just dump her. It's easy. You delete Laura's account, you don't reply to Alex's messages and you don't answer her calls or her texts. If you really want to make sure she leaves you alone, you can even change your mobile number – you could just tell everyone it was stolen. It's a hassle, but it would make Laura completely untraceable.'

'Yes,' I said. 'I can just pretend that Laura never existed. Alex will get over it, won't she? It's not like she and Laura were ever really close; we – they – had only met once. She'd be a bit confused, maybe a bit miffed for a while, and then she'd forget about me, I mean Laura, and get on with her life.'

'Exactly. And Jack will never find out. Absolutely no damage done.'

Katie made it sound so clean and simple, so easy. To her, erasing Alex from my life would be no greater an effort than crossing a name off a list. But that's all Alex was to her: a name. She hadn't spent time with her, talking to her and getting to know her. She hadn't met Alex's dad, or allowed him to buy her gifts. She didn't care about Alex's feelings.

I switched on my computer and prepared myself for the task of going straight into Laura's Topfriendz profile and deleting it. But by the time the login screen had come on I didn't feel so comfortable about doing that. Surely there must be a less cruel way of getting rid of Alex, a way to let her down gently? Maybe I could start by being really rude and objectionable, so that she'd begin to find me, I mean Laura, irritating or offensive and not want to be her friend any more. A series of fart gags might work, or a string of non-stop swear words, as if I'd suddenly developed Tourette's. I could come up with something terrible, like a racist or sexist remark that she couldn't ignore, something so nasty that no one in their right mind would tolerate. Perhaps I could deliberately cause a row over something . . . football, maybe? I could tell her I'd suddenly become a Tottenham Hotspur fan (which, for an Arsenal fan, would be the equivalent of becoming a suicide bomber) and she wouldn't want to speak to me again. My sudden personality change would shock her, but she'd either think I was a raving lunatic or that I now trusted her enough to reveal my true colours. Either way, she'd run a mile, relieved that she hadn't wasted any more time on Laura. Wouldn't that work just as well?

That approach didn't feel right, either. I know it sounds pathetic, but I didn't like the idea of Alex, or anyone, hating Laura or thinking badly of her. She was part of me, after all. I wondered if there was a way of just letting my friendship with Alex slide, of deliberately engineering it so that we drifted apart, just as I had with the girls I'd genuinely met and befriended at summer camp. I could be slack in answering Alex's messages, not phone when I said I would and forget to return her calls. Eventually, she'd grow fed up with chasing me and wonder why we'd ever become friends. No one would be hurt; nobody would hate anyone. It was the perfect solution. But how long would it take? Weeks? Months? Would I be able to hide it from Jack in the meantime? What if Alex was persistent and refused to let our friendship go? What if she turned into Laura's stalker . . . ?

As Laura's profile page downloaded, I was shocked to see what a mess it looked. Since I'd started talking to Alex I hadn't done anything to update it, and it had grown out of control, like an abandoned forest. I had about a million new friend requests, there were pop-ups and adverts everywhere and someone had posted a string of rude videos on my message board. It needed serious pruning. I wondered if you could employ web gardeners to do the job for you.

There were five messages in my inbox, two of which were from the ever-persistent Igor, one from the Topfriendz administrator and one from a band inviting me to buy their latest EP. The last message had been sent only a couple of hours earlier. It was from Alex.

*Hi Laura.*

*It was so lovely to see you earlier. Wasn't the match brill? I had such a fun afternoon and I really hope you did too. My dad thinks you're great – which you should take as a major compliment, because he hardly ever likes my friends – and he says you must come to another match with us soon, if you'd like to, of course. I'm going to have a party for my eighteenth birthday in a few weeks, which you must*

*come to, if you can. I'd love you to meet some of my other*
*friends.*

*Anyway, speak soon.*

*Love Alex xxx*

I found myself smiling, involuntarily. Alex was so warm and so sweet, wasn't she? Her message was lovely. She said she'd had a great time with me and, when I thought about it, I'd had a great time at the match too, in a way. I was certain it wasn't like thinking about an exam in retrospect and deciding it wasn't so bad after all. I genuinely had had fun. What's more, what Alex said was so flattering. She obviously really liked me, even though – unbeknown to her – I'd been at my worst all afternoon: dressed horribly, acting stupid, holding my tongue. Her dad liked me too, and she said he didn't like *any* of her friends. Perhaps, I thought, I simply can't help being naturally charming and likable, even in disguise.

'I can't dump Alex,' I said aloud, even though there was no one awake to hear me. 'I don't want to. I like her.'

I couldn't do it. I couldn't hurt Alex. It was too cruel. If Laura vanished off the face of the earth, there might be terrible repercussions for Alex. She would feel abandoned, betrayed, confused . . . She might never be able to trust anyone again. It could ruin her life, for ever. What if she reported Laura's disappearance to the police and there was a full-scale murder enquiry? What if she went mad because nobody believed her and ended her days in a hospital, dribbling and blathering on to the nurses about a missing girl called Laura Thompson, whom everybody said had never existed?

While I didn't want to hurt Alex, if I'm honest, that was only part of it: it was mainly about me. I couldn't delete Laura because I didn't want my little adventure to end yet. Before Alex, I hadn't made a new friend in ages. I knew everybody in my class at school and Sixth Form college was over a year away. I was bored. Alex could introduce me to new people, and teach me new things. Maybe spending time with her would make me sporty and fit too. Not that I could imagine doing any actual exercise with her, but who's to say it wouldn't happen naturally, like catching a cold, if I hung around her for long enough?

I still didn't know why she and Jack had broken up and I had no guarantee that Jack would ever tell me. Alex could fill in the gaps so I wouldn't keep bugging him about it. If I tried really, really hard, I could almost convince myself that it would be good for our relationship. As long as Jack didn't find out what I'd been up to, there was no reason why I couldn't be a loyal girlfriend to him and a good friend to Alex. Everyone has secrets; I'm sure I read somewhere that it's healthy to hold a few things back.

Maybe, one day, when we were firm friends (I hadn't determined quite how our friendship would become legitimate, but I'd worry about that another time), I'd be able to tell Alex the truth. By then, she wouldn't mind because she'd know I was trustworthy and a good person. And how, in the future, we'd laugh about the way we had met. How ridiculous it would seem. I imagined us twenty years on, when we we'd be really old, sitting around a dinner table, with my husband Jack (who would be a successful sports reporter with his own TV show and the best celebrity party invites), and whoever Alex married (for some reason, in my fantasy her husband had a beard), talking about our youth.

'I can't believe Lily changed her name and pretended to be someone else!' Alex would say.

'I know! What was she like!' Jack would reply. 'That's my Lily for you.' He'd laugh and squeeze my hand, and I'd stroke the swirly, whirly bit on the top of his head, which still wouldn't lie flat and was now streaked with silver.

'I think the name you used began with an "L" . . .' Alex would say. 'Lisa? Leah? No, Laura, wasn't it? Yes, that's right. Could you pass the wine please, Laura. Ha ha!'

And we'd all fall about.

Twenty years in the past, I sat alone in my bedroom and told myself everything would work out fine. Then I read Alex's message again, pressed the reply button and typed:

*It was so lovely to see you too. And to meet your dad. Tell him thanks again for the scarf. I'd love to come to your party and meet your friends. Let's speak v. soon.*

*Love Laura xxxx*

Before I went to bed, I texted Katie: *Laura nt dead. Wl xplain. Sorry xx*

I waited for about ten minutes, hoping we might chat about it, but she didn't reply. That wasn't like her. I told myself she must have been asleep.

# Chapter 14

♡

When I next saw Jack, two days after the night of revelations, he turned up at my house, unexpectedly, with a present.

'This is for you,' he said, nervously, even before I'd fully opened the front door. He pushed a small package wrapped in shiny 'Many Happy Returns' paper into my hands and gave me a clumsy kiss. The wrapping was clearly second hand, a leftover from someone's birthday, because I could see faded marks from old sticky tape on one side. 'I'm sorry about the wrapping,' he added, with an embarrassed grin. 'I mean the balloons and stuff. I do know it's not your birthday for months – I just couldn't find any other paper.'

'That's OK,' I said. 'I mean, oh my God. I mean, thank you.'

I was surprised, in a good way. Jack had never given me

a present before or, to be more accurate, he had never given me any present you can't find on the confectionary shelves in the newsagent ('I was buying a Snickers bar and thought you might like a Twirl' or 'Here, I saved you my last Rolo'). Certainly not a gift-wrapped, 'I've put some thought into this' present. I wasn't sure if he wanted me to open it in front of him, or save it for later. I squeezed it between my fingers and traced its outline in my palm, trying, inconspicuously, to work out what was it was, and whether I'd like it, so I could prepare my reaction. It had hard corners, like a box, and there was something inside that rattled.

'Go on then, open it,' he said, with anxious impatience.

'Yay!' I grinned. 'I was hoping you'd say that. Hang on . . .'

We were still standing in the hall, leaning against the radiator. I motioned towards the living room and he followed me inside. We both perched on the edge of the sofa, as I fumbled with the wrapping paper. He'd put so much sticky tape on that it took me ages to find an opening. When I did, the paper came away in strips, revealing a blue, lidded cardboard box. Lying inside was a silver bracelet covered in turquoise and pink sparkly stones, which were arranged in the shapes of flowers and stars.

'Oh my God, thank you, Jack,' I said. 'It's gorgeous.'

It was lovely. OK, maybe it wasn't the colours I'd have chosen for myself – I think gold looks better on me than silver, but boys don't tend to know about colours and skin tones and undertones, do they? – but it was really pretty, nonetheless. Jack had obviously taken some notice of my taste, because it wasn't too delicate, or too girly, but solid and chunky, with a sturdy clasp that made a satisfying clicking noise when you closed it. Kerlick. And opened it. Kerlick. And closed it again.

Jack appeared relieved. His shoulders relaxed and he smiled. 'I didn't buy it for you just because you gave me the scarf,' he said, which was silly, because I hadn't thought of that explanation until he suggested it. 'I was planning to get you it, anyway. I saw it and I thought you'd like it, and Ruth said you would. I wanted to give you something to show you how special you are to me.'

'Thank you,' I said. 'Thanks so much.' I forced a smile. It's not that I wasn't happy, but I didn't feel special, just confused and guilty. Jack put his arms around me and I felt grateful that when you hug someone you can't see each other's faces. 'Thank you again,' I said, my mouth pressed into his back . 'I really do like it.'

He kissed me and I allowed him to put the bracelet on my wrist. It glittered gorgeously under the spotlights, even though the stones clashed horribly with my brown and red school uniform. Mind you, pretty much everything clashes with that.

'I like you a lot, Lily,' Jack said. 'I wanted you to know that.'

'I like you a lot too, Jack.'

Jack's mission completed, he went home shortly afterwards and so I didn't have the chance to ask him any of the questions that had been collecting in my head since he'd told me about his dad. I didn't get the opportunity the following weekend either, and it didn't seem right to talk about it on the phone, when we only ever had a few minutes, and there were always other people around.

Two weeks went by and still Jack hadn't mentioned his dad again. If I'd imagined that on the night he'd told me he had chosen to open a door and let me in to snoop around in his past, I was dead wrong. It turned out I was the kind of visitor you invite to wait in the porch but don't allow to come into the actual house. By not asking all my questions that night – which would have been impossible, given that I hadn't thought of them then – I'd unwittingly missed my chance to uncover any more details. Now the door was bolted shut. Whenever I tried to bring up his dad or his childhood, Jack would change the subject, just like before. Each time I pressed him, he'd tell me, sweetly, that he didn't want to talk about it: I knew everything anyone needed to know and the matter should stay in the past where it belonged. He'd say things like, 'It's not who I am any more, Lily,' or 'It's me and you, right now, that matter, not what happened five years ago.' And although he never actually said he wished he hadn't told me, I could see he was thinking it. If we were watching TV together and one of those 'Stop child cruelty' adverts came on, he'd shuffle around awkwardly, not looking me in the eye, while I'd cringe inwardly and pretend I hadn't noticed. It was almost as uncomfortable as sitting through a movie sex scene with my parents.

It eventually dawned on me that Jack hadn't told me about his dad for my benefit at all, even if he'd made it seem that way. Whatever he said, he hadn't done it to bring us closer, or because he thought I needed to know, or because it would help me to understand him. He'd done it to make himself feel better, like a bulimic throwing up when they've gorged on a secret stash of cakes and sweets. After he'd purged himself of his secret, he felt ashamed and wanted to pretend it hadn't happened. I began to wonder if he'd given me the bracelet to buy my silence. When I put it on, it felt tight and restrictive, like one of those tags that criminals have to wear. Kerlick.

*The fitting of this bracelet means that you are now electronically tagged, Miss Lily Lawton, and if you ask any difficult or deeply personal questions an alarm will sound at the police station and you will be taken directly to jail. Do you understand?*

Katie said I should be satisfied that Jack been honest about his dad at last. 'Drop it,' she warned. 'You know Jack's big secret now, plus you know he really cares for you. Stop worrying about his waste of space dad. He doesn't. And so what if he said Alex finished with him when it was the other way round? It's not against the law. I don't get what more you want from him. If you keep going on and on about it he'll just get pissed off.'

Part of me knew she was right, but I also knew she was still sore at me for not breaking off contact with Alex and fed up with the whole business. What she really wanted was for things to go back to the way they used to be, when it was just the two of us, fooling around and hanging out together. No boys, no complications. Sometimes, I felt I wanted that too. Life was undeniably simpler and a lot less stressful before I met Jack and Alex.

But, try as I might, I couldn't stop thinking about Jack's dad. I suppose it was almost becoming an obsession, although I wouldn't have admitted that. It was certainly weird; I'd never been particularly interested in anybody else's parents. They don't tend to be all that fascinating. Normal parents have three basic modes: tired, hassled or angry; and if you try to talk to them, they don't listen properly. You have to tolerate them and be polite to them because they come as part of the package with your friends or boyfriends. And they can be useful for food and for lifts.

Jack's dad was different. He was one hundred per cent a *bad* man, and that made him intriguing. I'd never known anyone truly bad before. Sure, I'd met people who did bad things – playground bullies and people who lied and stole things from shops – and, let's face it, I'm hardly Snow White

– but I'd never knowingly met a wicked person. I wanted to know what he looked like, whether he had an evil aura. Was he a big man? Did he have muscles and tattoos? What did his voice sound like? Was it gruff and deep? Could you tell he was cruel just by looking in his eyes? I also wondered if any of his badness could have leaked into Jack. Even if he hadn't directly inherited it, they'd lived together for twelve years, which was more than long enough for some of it to have seeped in through his pores. Maybe he didn't even realise it was there. People always tell me I'm like my dad, even though I can't see it.

I decided to see if I could find Jack's dad on the internet. All I knew was that he was called Mr Mullins and that he was a teacher, so I put 'Mr Mullins' and 'teacher' into Google. It turned out there were tons of teachers called Mullins; perhaps, for some reason, it's one of those names that influences what you do, even if you aren't aware of it, like being called Mr Payne and becoming a dentist. I didn't know his first name, so I couldn't narrow my search that way, but I did know that Jack had lived in Milton Keynes. Was his dad still there? Had he taught at a local school? I searched again, this time adding 'Milton Keynes' to my keywords. Now there was only one result: a profile of a Mr David Mullins, 'a headteacher with over twenty years experience in the profession' – including in Milton Keynes – from a school in Luton. Was he Jack's dad? Above it was a small, black and white photograph showing a balding man in glasses, with a warm smile. There was something familiar about his expression, the slight lopsidedness of his grin, that made me certain I'd found my man. I stared at the picture for a few minutes, trying to glean something from it. But the man's face didn't tell me anything; it certainly didn't radiate evil and it wasn't the face of a monster. His eyes didn't follow me around the room and his teeth didn't transform into dagger-sharp fangs. He looked average, normal, dull, like the next old guy in a suit. He could have been anyone.

Whoever had written his profile (although I suppose he could have written it himself) thought very highly of him:

*Mr David Mullins has been the headteacher at Mountview High for the past two years and has helped to cement the school's reputation for academic and sporting excellence. Before taking up this position, he enjoyed an illustrious career as a teacher and as a deputy head at schools in Milton Keynes and throughout Buckinghamshire. Prior to becoming a teacher, he studied chemistry at Manchester University and he retains a keen interest in the subject. In 2008, he initiated the school's 'Young Chemist' award for children who have shown an aptitude for science. He lives in Luton with his wife and young child . . .*

I gasped. His what? His wife and young child? Did Jack even know his dad had married again? Was he aware he had a half brother or sister he'd never met? Did he know that his dad lived in Luton? And if he didn't know all this, should I tell him? I toyed with this possibility for a few minutes. If I did, Jack would find out I'd been secretly investigating his dad, but there's no law against Googling someone. I'd be doing him a favour, wouldn't I? It could help him to come to terms with everything. Surely, if his dad had a whole new life, he wouldn't stalk Jack's family any more. Maybe he'd changed for the better.

But what if he hadn't? What if he hit his new wife too? My heart began to pound. Did anybody know what he was really like? Shouldn't someone report him? I imagined a classroom of Year Sevens chanting in unison, 'Good morning, Mr Mullins', unaware that after breakfast that morning he'd punched his wife in the stomach, and it made me shiver.

There was an email address on the profile, for people who wanted to contact the school, and I mulled over the idea of writing an anonymous email to Mr Mullins, telling him I knew his secret and that he was being watched. But then I figured, if he's so darn good at science he's probably good on the internet too, and he would find a way of tracing me, and that might put Jack and his mum in danger. So I thought better of it.

That night, for the first time in years, I dreamed that the Bogeyman was hiding under my bed. He was hairy and green, with a slightly lopsided grin.

# Chapter 15

♡

*Topfriendz*
*Inbox: 2 messages*
*Message One*
*From: Igor*
*Subject: Hello*
*Hello lovely ladee,*
*You no likey make talk? Write me please soon. I mees*
*you much.*
*Love and kisez*
*Igor x*

*Message Two*
*From: Alex*
*Subject: Parteeee!!!*

*Hi Laura,*

*Hope you can still come to my birthday party next weekend. I've got this awesome new top – can't wait for you to see it! And I meant to say, you are bringing Jared, aren't you – obviously he's invited too and I'm dying to meet him. Give me a call so we can sort all the arrangements.*

*Love Alex xxx*

Alex's party: I'd put it to the back of my mind for as long as I could, but now it was only days away and I could no longer avoid thinking about it. I was sure Alex's top was lovely, but I had far bigger worries than what to wear. The prospect of taking Laura out in public again was bad enough; worse was the matter of how I'd deal with the Jared situation (or rather, my lack of a Jared situation). In my opinion, Jared's non-existence made him the very worst kind of party pooper. Why had Alex decided to invite him too? Why did she always have to do the right thing, the polite thing? Still, I could see that not extending the invite to my 'boyfriend' would have been a bit weird, especially when she asked about him all the time, and when I seemed so devoted to him. I'd even told her I saw Jared every weekend, so she probably thought I'd expected he could come.

If only she'd suggested that he was invited when she'd first mentioned the party, I could have said he had something important planned, like a holiday. Now, it was too late, I'd have to think of another excuse. It would be unconvincing to invent a last-minute bargain so tempting that his parents would think, what the hell, and take him out of college in the middle of term.

In soaps, when they want to get rid of a character quickly, unseen, they generally either kill them off in a tragic, off-stage accident or they make the doomed character win the lottery and decide to leave the country. Neither of those options would work for me. If Jared 'died' I'd hardly be in the mood for partying, while, if he won the lottery, all he'd want to do was party. In fact, he'd be up for the biggest celebration of his life, with me, Alex and the world. That's if he actually existed, obviously.

One thing was clear: Jared wouldn't be coming with me to the party. Not unless I could persuade Katie to dress in drag and talk in a deep voice all evening, which I doubted. She'd make a rubbish bloke: she was too pretty and her boobs were too big. More to the point, she couldn't come with me; I needed her to be my alibi. She'd agreed, reluctantly, to let me tell my parents and Jack that I was staying at hers for the night. How else could I get away with it?

I felt like kicking myself (which I've always thought was a stupid expression. I've never seen anybody do it, literally. Wouldn't they just fall over?). Why couldn't I have told Alex I was single? Jared was a liability, I'd been thinking that for weeks. My lies about him were stacking up precariously; sometimes I couldn't remember what I'd told Alex, and I'm sure I contradicted myself frequently. I also didn't like having to keep lying to her about his exploits, his gigs and his injuries. I know that sounds ridiculous and hypocritical because my entire relationship with Alex was built on a huge lie, but most of what I told her day-to-day was the truth. The truth, with names changed and a few vital omissions.

I thought about ringing Katie to ask her advice, but decided against it. Ever since the night when I'd chosen not to break off contact with Alex, I'd felt awkward talking to Katie about her. Maybe I was being oversensitive, but I got the impression she was judging me and that she'd say any subsequent problem or issue I had was of my own making. I was aware that I'd stopped telling her every last detail of Alex's emails and calls. Partly, it was because I didn't think they'd interest her, but it was also because I didn't like Katie's negativity, the way she always seemed to want to put Alex down. Most of what Alex and I chatted about would have bored her senseless. Why did it matter to Katie if Alex had bought a new CD, or that she'd decided to go to a music festival in the summer? And why would Katie have been interested in the fact that Alex was really starting to like a guy called Ben in her economics class? So, whenever she asked if I'd heard from Alex, I'd say, yes, she messaged me, or she emailed me, and we'd leave it at that.

Still, I wasn't used to making big decisions without Katie's help. What could I do about Jared? How could I make him go away? Perhaps I could tell Alex I'd dumped him. It seemed highly unlikely that in twenty-four hours I could go from being super loved-up to over him, for no reason. Could he have dumped me? That was a better option: it was feasible I might not have seen it coming and I'd be entitled to be so upset that I didn't want to talk about it in too much depth. Lying about being dumped seemed to work for Jack, I thought, bitterly, so why not for me too?

*Hi Alex,* I typed. I know she'd asked me to call but, despite all the practice I'd had, making up tall tales was still much easier – and somehow felt less wrong – on screen.

*I'm really looking forward to coming to your party but I won't be bringing Jared. I'm crying while I write this because the skank dumped me last night. I was going to tell you but I really haven't felt like talking about it. He said he didn't think things were working out and we were getting too serious. I don't think he's going to change his mind – there's this other girl . . . I don't want to think about it. I miss him so much.*

*I promise I'll call you when I feel a bit better.*

*Love Laura xx*

Didn't that sound authentic? Especially the 'crying while I write this' bit. Technically, I reasoned, this wasn't a lie at all. You can't lie about something that was untrue in the first place, can you? Jared had never been my boyfriend, so it wasn't physically possible to be dumped by him. Isn't there a rule about two negatives making a positive? Maybe if you tell two lies they cancel each other out. Maybe telling two lies creates a truth . . . I'm not entirely sure where I was going with this train of thought, but it made me feel better about things.

Alex's reply, which arrived almost instantly, was as sweet as I anticipated:

*Hi Laura,*

*Really sorry to hear about Jared. I know how much you liked him. Whenever you want to talk about it, let me know. I'll understand if you don't want to come to my party anymore, but if you do, and I really hope you will, I promise all my friends will cheer you up and you'll have an ace time.*

*Love Alex xxxxx*

There was no way I was missing the party, not when I'd done so much planning to be there. I know that only a week before I'd have done practically anything to get out of going, but now I was almost looking forward to it. My curiosity was pulling me there, like a magnet. I'd just have to show Alex how strong and how brave I could be. Goodness, I was practically over Jared already.

*Hi Alex,*

*Thanks for being so understanding.*

*I'll be OK. I keep telling myself he was only a guy – I'm not going to let him get me down. He was way too skinny anyway. And I'm definitely still coming to your party. I'm really looking forward to it. I promise I won't sit in the corner looking miserable.*

*I've just had a double chocolate muffin and I'm feeling better already. I'll call you about arrangements.*

*Love Laura xxx*

*P.S. Jared who?*

So there it was: Jared was no more.

In the moment after I'd pressed send, it struck me that I was really going to miss having a boyfriend who played in a band, even if it was an imaginary one.

# chapter 16

♡

*Have you ever climbed on a bicycle and set off happily down the road, only to find that the brakes don't work, and you're at the top of a hill? As you career down, faster and faster, you grip on to the handlebars for dear life, waiting for a soft patch of grass or sand pit to present itself so you can leap to safety. But you hesitate because you know jumping off will really hurt and you're going so fast that everything is a blur, and so you keep holding on hoping that, maybe, when you reach the bottom of the hill, you'll come to a natural stop and everything will be all right.*

*And then you crash.*

Alex's house is right on the other side of London, where there isn't even a tube. She lives in a place that shouldn't really be called London at all; the city has sprawled out towards it and it clings on by its fingernails. To reach it, I had to get a bus, a proper train and then another bus, and door-to-door it took me almost two hours. I'd never travelled so far or for so long on my own before and I felt quite proud that I made all my connections and didn't have to ask anyone for directions. Of course, I'd never be able to tell anyone about my journey; only Katie knew where I was that day. It would serve me right, I thought, if there was an accident or if a terrorist blew up the train, and nobody worried about me. I didn't even have any ID on me, so if Alex reported me missing first, the police would look for someone called Laura Thompson. There wouldn't be any records and Alex would have to identify me. What if my parents never found out the truth? I might be buried as Laura Thompson and there'd be no one to visit my grave . . .

'You're taking a lot of stuff to stay at Katie's,' Mum had commented, before I left. 'Doesn't she already have a sleeping bag?'

'It's in the wash,' I'd said, without pause for breath. I'd predicted this line of questioning. 'It got mud on it from camping. And I'm taking a load of clothes for Katie and some of our other friends to try on – she's having a clothes swapping party.'

The truth was that I had packed half my wardrobe because I couldn't decide what Laura should wear to Alex's party. Tracky bums wouldn't do this time, that was certain, but beyond that, I was clueless. Laura needed an image overhaul. Maybe I'd ask Alex for a makeover before the party. That was a good idea: I could see what her party clothes were like and then borrow one of her dresses, and beg her to do my hair and make-up, just like hers. Not that she seemed like the type of girl to worry about her hair and make-up – she might be hopeless at it. Still, I'd ask her anyway. If nothing else, she'd be flattered. My final appearance mattered far less than retaining some element of disguise. If I looked and felt too much like myself, I might slip back into being Lily.

There was one element of Laura's persona that I had prepared for in advance: her short-sightedness. If she knew she would be staying over at Alex's, Laura would have brought her glasses. I really couldn't 'forget' them again. On my way to the station, I'd stopped off at a trendy shop on the high street where I knew they sold fashion glasses (the type that are clear glass and meant purely for posing), and bought the cheapest pair I could find. They were purple, too large and totally the wrong shape for my face, giving me the look of Elton John in the seventies. He was doing a lot of drugs at the time, so at least he had an excuse.

'They look cool,' said the shop assistant in a 'can't be bothered' manner, when I asked for his opinion. He had looked me up and down and dismissed me the moment I walked through the door. 'The colour matches your eyes.'

For the record, I don't have purple eyes. I'd call them brown, with a few hazel flecks. You could even get away with caramel, if you were trying to be descriptive. Maybe he was colour blind, as well as pretentious.

'Thanks,' I said, brightly. 'I'll take them.' I made a mental note never to return to that shop. I don't like people who lie through their teeth.

Yes, alright, I know.

Alex's house was only about a hundred metres from the bus stop, which was a relief, given the amount I was carrying. I stood outside for few minutes, breathing deeply and trying to compose myself. Laura is just a name, I told myself. You've pulled it off once, you can do it again. A man on the other side of the street stared at me, suspiciously. I waved at him and he turned away, pretending he hadn't noticed.

Alex had invited me to come early, so I could settle in and feel at home before the party, and not feel overwhelmed by her friends. 'It's easier to meet new people one at a time, rather than walking into a room full of strangers,' she'd said, thoughtfully. 'Plus,' she'd added, 'it would be useful to have another pair of hands to help set up.' It had seemed like a good idea when she suggested it, but now I realised it meant more time being Laura, and under the scrutiny of her parents too, and I felt anxious. I wondered if I should put the glasses on right away, but I didn't want to frighten anyone. Instead, I pulled my hair back into Laura's customary ponytail, took a deep breath, stood up straight (sporty Laura had much better posture than me, I'd decided) and rang the doorbell.

Alex's Dad opened the front door. 'Hello Laura, it's good

to see you,' he said. He glanced at my bags, before picking one of them up. 'My goodness, you have brought a lot with you. Are you planning to move in with us?'

I reddened. 'No, Mr Porter, and thank you very much for having me. I just wasn't sure what to bring.'

'It's OK, Laura, I was only teasing. I'll take your bags up to Alex's room. Why don't you go into the kitchen – Alex is in there with her mother.' He pointed to his left, and called out, 'Alex, your guest is here!'

She came out of the kitchen, smiling. There was something different about her, something I couldn't quite figure out.

'Hi Laura,' she said. 'I'm so glad you made it. How are you feeling? Come in and have a drink. We're just sorting out some food for tonight.' She gave me a hug and took me by the arm, leading me into the room behind her.

'I know – it's your hair!' I exclaimed (after I said hello, of course). 'You've had your hair cut! It really suits you.' She'd had her hair styled into a long bob, which gave it more body and made it seem glossier. She looked lovely, older and more groomed, and our two-year age difference all at once felt more stark to me. I'd never been to an eighteenth birthday party before; only a few of my friends had turned sixteen. People always said I appeared and acted grown-up for my age; would anyone guess I was still only fifteen (and three-quarters)?

'Thanks,' Alex said, stroking the ends of her hair, in the

way that people do when they're not used to a new style. 'I fancied a change. Mum, meet Laura.'

Alex's mum came over. She was much shorter and rounder than Alex, with a kind face.

'Hello Laura,' she said, in a soft Scottish accent. 'I've heard so much about you.' She held up her hands, which were covered in flour and butter, and laughed. 'Do you mind if we don't shake just now?'

We spent the next two hours baking and icing cupcakes, something I hadn't done since I was a kid. I'd forgotten how much fun it could be, especially the decorating part. My cupcakes were works of art, with marbled technicolour icing and jelly tots and silver balls arranged so prettily that they'd have made Nigella proud. The only problem was, they looked so good I decided I didn't want anybody to eat them. I said someone should set up a cupcake gallery so I could put them on display.

Alex's mum laughed at me. 'I didn't buy all those ingredients just so they could go mouldy in a museum somewhere. Trust me, they'll taste even better than they look.'

She was right. By the time Alex and I went upstairs to get ourselves ready for the party, I'd eaten so many cupcakes that I wasn't sure Laura would fit into any of Alex's dresses, or mine.

Alex's bedroom was right at the top of the house, in a converted loft. It was incredibly neat and clean, which I should have expected, with Arsenal posters all over the walls. A scarf, just like the one her dad had bought me – and that I'd passed on to Jack – hung above her bed. It looked more like a boy's bedroom than a girl's.

'Thanks for letting me stay,' I said.

'No worries, it'll be good to spend some proper time together. And there's no way you'd have been able to get home on your own tonight to . . . where is it that you live again?'

'North London,' I said, narrowing it down to about a twenty-mile area. I'd always been deliberately vague about the exact location of my house, because it was where Jack lived too, and I wasn't sure if Alex knew his new address. Realising I might sound evasive, I added, 'Um, a couple of miles from the Arsenal ground.'

'Oh yeah, that's right. You're so lucky! I'd love to come and visit you some time soon.'

'Definitely,' I said, hoping she couldn't hear the insincerity in my voice. 'We'll have to arrange it.' Of course, if we were going to be proper friends, I'd have to find a way around this problem too, even if it meant setting up in a squat on my own, or paying for Jack to leave the country.

'Let me give you your present,' I said, changing the subject. I'd bought Alex a CD she'd mentioned she wanted, by some girl band I didn't rate. It didn't seem like much for an eighteenth, so I'd added a set of rose perfumed soaps and body lotion from Mum's spare present collection, which was mainly made up of recycled gifts. Mum always said she worried that one day she'd end up giving an unwanted present back to the person who'd bought it for her.

'Thanks!' Alex exclaimed. 'Ooh, exciting. Do you mind if I open it on my actual birthday?'

I shook my head. I was relieved. It's always embarrassing when someone has to pretend they like your gift, when they don't.

'We should get ready,' said Alex. 'I've cleared some space for you over there, if you want to sort your stuff out.'

I unpacked my bags and laid out all my things. Alex came over to take a look.

'Are those your glasses?'

'Yes,' I said. I screwed my nose up. 'Hideous, aren't they?'

'Hmm, I can see why you don't like them. They're pretty big. Whatever possessed you to get purple?'

Because they matched my eyes? 'They were in the sale,' I said.

'Here, let me try them . . .'

Before I could stop her, Alex had put on my comedy glasses. Far too large for her, they slid straight down her nose, where they perched precariously. She looked about fifty in them. Fifty and completely batty.

'They're not very strong,' she said. 'I can see perfectly through them and I've got my lenses in. I thought you said you were really short sighted.'

'Maybe you need a new prescription,' I suggested. 'They make a big difference to me.'

She frowned. 'Maybe.'

Using Alex for a makeover proved to be a nonstarter. Clearly, I couldn't ask her to do my hair like hers, not unless she'd suddenly acquired the skills of Nicky Clarke. And her idea of make-up, even for a party, was a dab of lip-gloss and some clear mascara. I wear more than that to school. As for her dresses: she didn't have any. Not a single one. Her party outfit was a pair of jeans and a red long-sleeved T-shirt with sequins scattered across it.

'Your new top is lovely,' I said. It wasn't something I'd have worn, but it suited her. 'I don't know what to wear at all. Can you help?' I pulled four dresses – every single one that I possessed – out of my rucksack. 'What do you think?'

Alex rifled through them, holding each one up to the light and measuring it up against me. 'They're all really nice. But I'm not a dress or skirt person. I never get my legs out, so I'm probably not the person to ask.'

'You've got great, shapely legs,' I said. I was being genuine.

'Nah, they're too muscley. You're lucky yours haven't bulked up through exercise. My calves are bigger than my dad's.'

Yet another reason not to exercise, I thought. Who wants calves like a man?

'Why don't you go for the green one?' Alex suggested.

'It's the nicest colour and I like the square neckline.'

'Thanks,' I said. 'Good choice.' It's funny that she'd picked out the green jersey dress; it was the one I'd never worn because I didn't feel entirely comfortable in it. I'd liked it in the shop but every time I put it on at home I took it straight off again. It wasn't quite me. Maybe that's because it was more Laura.

'You seem a lot happier than I thought you'd be,' Alex said, as we finished getting dressed. 'I thought you'd be all puffy eyed and quiet, but you're totally being yourself. Are you really OK about Jared?'

'I'm fine,' I said. I tried to make myself look sad. Until she'd mentioned Jared I'd forgotten that I was meant to be heartbroken. In fact, I was so relaxed I hadn't been acting at all. 'Honestly. It's nice of you to ask, but I don't really want to talk about it, or I'll get upset.'

'Sure. Sorry.' She put her hand on my shoulder. 'Anytime you want to, let me know.'

'Course,' I said. 'Now, let's party!'

# Chapter 17

♡

Alex's parents thoughtfully took themselves out for the night at about seven, and the first party guests started arriving at eight. Alex said she was expecting about forty people (assuming nobody had posted an open invite up on Topfriendz), mostly college friends and a few selected friends from her sports and drama clubs. She said she couldn't wait to introduce me to her best friend Jessica ('I've told her so much about you') and to Ben, the guy from her economics class whom she thought had potential, and about whom she wanted my honest opinion.

While we'd been getting ready, Alex's parents had transformed the house. The lights had been dimmed and there were multicoloured fairy lights strung up across the living room and hall, giving everything a hazy glow. There were balloons and 'Happy Eighteenth' banners stuck to every wall and in the corner of the living room stood two huge tables covered in food and drink, including a bowl of fruit punch so large that a child could have had a bath in it. As it was her eighteenth, Alex's parents had given her a few bottles of champagne to celebrate with, the remainder of the drinks being soft.

I hung around in the background while Alex greeted her guests, smiling and waving hello each time she pointed me out. When Ben arrived, Alex gave me a wink. I hadn't expected him to resemble Jack, but he had the same stocky build and fairish hair, and it unnerved me. Either Alex had a 'type' or she was even less over Jack than I'd thought. I forced a grin and winked back, nodding my head in approval.

I didn't warm to Jessica. I felt that she eyed me suspiciously when we were introduced and that she'd made up her mind in advance to dislike me. Like Katie, she was clearly jealous when anybody new appeared on the scene and extremely protective of her best friend. I decided to keep my distance. The last thing I needed was somebody asking too many probing questions.

Being Laura at the party was easy. I discovered that if you dance a lot, you don't really have to talk to people at all, you can just smile at them. Even when people did try to make smalltalk, the music was so loud nobody could hear what anyone else was saying. This guy – his name sounded like Steve or Dave – kept dancing next to me and trying to make eye contact. Every time he came too close I twirled my body around, so that I was dancing with my back to him. That was very rude of Laura; of course, Lily would never do anything like that.

I spent a great deal of time hovering by the food and drinks table, keeping busy by rearranging the cupcakes (hiding the best ones at the back in the hopes they'd be left over at the end) and pouring myself punch. I was hungry but nobody else was eating much and I didn't want to look like a greedy pig, so I stuck to crisps and nuts, which I could stuff into my mouth while nobody was looking. As there was lots of fruit in the punch I figured it would count towards my five a day.

I wasn't expecting it, but I really started to enjoy myself. The weird thing was, I lost all track of time. I'd be dancing and then I'd look at my watch and a whole hour would have gone by. And maybe I did need glasses after all, because I was sure the room was starting to go a bit blurry, and that when people talked to me their voices sounded echoey and that they were swaying backwards and forwards. Even stranger, my thoughts were all jumbled up and seemed to be popping into my head in a random order. When the room began to swim, I stumbled to the door and announced, 'Feeling a bit dizzy,' to no one in particular. Somehow, I managed to find my way out through the kitchen into the back garden. I sat smack down on the patio and almost rolled straight over. I giggled, righted myself, looked around me and then remembered how Jack and I had first met during a party, in a back garden not dissimilar to this one. I found myself smiling in a moronic way. Oh my God, I thought. I feel totally out of control. I must be pissed. I've never been pissed before. But I've only drunk fruit punch. How did that happen?

I don't know how long I'd been outside, when Alex came to find me. 'Are you OK?' she asked. 'Someone said they'd seen you come outside. Here . . .' She handed me a pint glass full of water. 'Drink this.'

'I juscht needed some fresch air,' I slurred, taking the glass and spilling half of it. 'I'll be finesh.'

'Oh dear. Sorry,' she said. 'I should have warned you. Someone poured a load of vodka and God knows what else in the punch. Don't tell my parents – they'll freak.'

'Shokay.'

'By the way, I promised I'd tell you this: my friend Dave really likes you. You know, the dark guy who was dancing with you for a while. He thinks you're playing hard to get. I told him you just broke up with someone and it's probably too soon. Am I right?'

I nodded, although I didn't have complete control of my head, so it might have been a shake. 'I still love Jasch . . .' I heard the name 'Jack' begin to tumble out of my mouth, as if in slow motion, but I couldn't stop myself. 'I . . . mean . . . Jaresch.' I giggled, hysterically. 'Whoops, I can't even shay it.'

'I know.' She smiled. She hadn't noticed my slip-up. 'I'm going to get you some food and another drink. Stay there.' It seemed only a second later that she was standing next to me with a plateful of bread and cheese and another pint of water. 'Have this, you'll feel better.'

'Thanksch.' I drank the glass of water down in one. I'd had no idea how thirsty I was.

As I sat guzzling, I noticed a strange buzzing sensation in my hip. It took me a while to compute that the vibrations were coming from my mobile phone, which was inside my clutch bag. I fumbled for it, with hands that didn't feel like they belonged to me. When I took it out, it was flashing, *J calling*. Jack! I felt a dull, slow panic rising in my chest. Why was Jack calling me now? What should I do?

'Aren't you going to answer that?' asked Alex.

'Yeshh, no, I dunno,' I slurred.

'Is it Jared?'

'Umm, yesssh.'

'You don't have to talk to him if you don't want to.' She put her arm around me and squeezed my shoulder. 'Call him back when you're ready to talk – and when you're sober is probably a good idea. Make him sweat.'

I pressed reject. *You have seven missed calls* read the display on my phone (at least I think it did – it may have been one or eleven – I was seeing double). Funny, I hadn't heard it ring once. I stared at the message for a minute, wondering what to do next. Then, because I wasn't thinking clearly, I switched the phone off and put it back inside my bag.

'Are you coming back in with me?'

'In a few minish.'

'OK, but I'm coming out to get you if you don't come back in soon. You'll freeze out here.'

'Thanksch Lau-ra,' I said.

She laughed. 'Silly. You're Laura, I'm Alex, remember.'

'Oh yesch. I'm Lau-ra. Lau-ra Tschompson.'

'That's right.' She gave me a sympathetic glance, like she'd decided there was no hope for me, and went back inside.

The cold and the food did help to sober me up, although when I realised how close I'd come to giving the game away I almost wished I were out of it again. Maybe, I thought, subconsciously, I want Alex to know the truth. But not like that; she couldn't find out like that. I gathered myself together, smoothing down my dress and combing my hair with my fingers. I could see my faint reflection in the patio doors. I looked a fright: most of my make-up had melted off and my eye liner had smudged under my eyes.

The party I went back into was the not same one I'd left. The food and drinks table had been desecrated and there were crisps and bits of cupcake spread across the carpet, which were gradually being kneaded into the fibres under people's shoes. In every corner couples were snogging and a few people had slumped asleep against the wall. I felt like a spare part. If I hadn't been staying at Alex's, this would have been the time to leave. But I couldn't leave. Where was she?

I saw her across the room. She was sitting with a group of people, holding hands with Ben, her head on his shoulder. Good for her, I thought. Perhaps I should make my excuses and go to bed? Before I could, she spotted me.

'Laura,' she called out. 'Come over here.' She beckoned to me. 'A few of us are going to play spin the bottle with one of the champagne bottles my parents gave me. Why don't you join us?'

'I don't know,' I said. Spin the bottle usually spelled trouble.

Jessica sidled up to me. 'Oh, go on. It will be fun.' She had a mischievous look in her eye.

Alex looked at me, wide-eyed. 'Please, Laura. Play with me. It is my birthday after all.'

What could I say? 'OK then.'

I wouldn't have agreed so readily had I known in advance that Dave was one of the players. He seemed very pleased indeed when I sat down in the circle opposite him.

'I think we should play the Truth or Dare version,' said Jessica. 'Here goes . . .' She spun the bottle hard, so that it revolved six or seven times before coming to rest with its thin end pointing in the direction of a plump girl named Sarah. 'Truth or dare?' she asked.

'Truth,' said Sarah, without hesitation. Evidently, she wasn't the adventurous type.

'OK. Do you fancy Robbie?'

Sarah went bright red. Clearly she did. 'Umm, er, yes,' she admitted. She tried, bashfully, to catch Robbie's gaze but he looked away and rolled his eyes at the girl sitting next to him. Poor Sarah.

'Hah!' said Jessica. 'I knew it! Your go to spin.'

Sarah's spin sent the bottle careering out of the circle. On her second attempt, it ended its journey at Alex, who chose 'dare'.

'I dare you to snog Ben,' said Sarah. Jessica groaned. It wasn't much of a dare, given that Alex and Ben had clearly been joined at the lips for most of the party. Alex was only too happy to oblige.

'Get a room, guys,' said Jessica. 'In normal circumstances, I'd make Sarah give you another dare, but as it's your party, I'll allow it. Just this once.'

Eventually, Alex pulled herself away from Ben and took her turn at spinning. The bottle pointed at a boy called Carl, who was dared to run around the garden in his boxers. Having done so, he spun and the bottle came to a stop right in front of me.

'Truth or dare?' he said.

I hesitated. Of course, you must be thinking that it's obvious what I did next. Why, you'd even put money on the fact that I said, 'Truth.' It makes no odds what the question might have been: given that my whole persona was a lie, I should easily have been able to tell another, and tell it well.

But I couldn't do it. Why not? Because some stupid superstition, some idiotic belief that there's a higher morality at work when playing spin the bottle, made me unable to risk answering a question I couldn't answer honestly. It was just like when I was a kid and someone asked me to swear on my mother's life that what I claimed was true. I simply couldn't do it, just in case I really did condemn her to a terrible end.

So I said, 'Dare.'

'But I don't know you,' said Carl. 'Someone else should come up with the dare.'

'I know . . .' volunteered Jessica. 'This is a good one. Laura, I dare you to snog Dave.'

I tried not to show my horror. Alex must have told Jessica that Dave liked me; she'd probably also told her that I'd just broken up with my boyfriend and was feeling very vulnerable. Now the cow was playing games with me. I wanted to say, 'I'd rather run round the garden naked,' but I didn't want to hurt Dave's feelings. I looked at Alex, my eyes pleading.

'Can't you make her do something else?' asked Alex. 'No offence to you Dave, but like I told you, Laura's literally just broken up with someone.'

'Oh yeah,' said Jessica. 'The boy from the band, wasn't it? No, I'm sorry. Rules are rules. And if they've broken up, she's free and single and she can snog anyone she likes.'

Dave grinned at me, nervously. He looked like someone

152

who knows they've won the lottery but can't find their winning ticket. 'Come on, just a quickie,' he said. 'I don't bite. Well, not usually.'

I could feel tears beginning to well up in my eyes. Despite all my lies, the one line I'd never crossed was cheating on Jack. Everything I'd done for our relationship; well, it started off that way, at least. How could I kiss another guy, even if it was just for a dare? Jack was very clear on what he considered cheating, and kissing someone else was a no go. If he found out, he'd never forgive me. I didn't even *want* to kiss anyone but Jack. But how could I get out of it? I couldn't say, 'Actually, I didn't split up with my boyfriend at all,' because then everyone would know I'd been dishonest. I couldn't tell the truth without exposing all my lies.

'OK,' I said. 'I'll do it.' I breathed deeply and tried to imagine that I – no Laura – was a spy on a treacherous mission, forced to seduce an evil man in order to save her lover's life. Then I crawled over to Dave, grabbed him by the shoulders and, as quickly as I could, gave him a hard smack of a kiss on the mouth. No tongues. No soft lips. Barely any contact. When I pulled back Dave looked dazed and a little annoyed.

'That's not a snog,' Jessica griped.

'Leave her alone, Jess,' said Alex, her tone concerned. She could see how upset I looked. That only made me feel worse.

'I think I'm going to go to bed now,' I said, clambering up from the floor, before anyone could argue with my decision. 'Goodnight everyone.'

I managed to leave the room and make it halfway up the stairs before bursting into tears. About ten minutes later, Alex came up to see if I was all right, but I pretended I was already asleep.

I lay awake for what felt like hours, staring into the dark, my mind racing. I heard the front door slam several times as people left, and there were low murmured voices when Alex's parents arrived home. At some point Alex came to bed and, exhausted, fell asleep almost at once.

At about three a.m., I remembered that I'd turned off my mobile phone hours earlier, without listening to my voicemail. I tiptoed into the bathroom and switched it back on, hoping that it wouldn't wake Alex. There was a text from Katie, three message alerts and about a dozen missed calls. Katie's text read *Cl me now!!!* She hadn't ended it with kisses, which was unusual and rather an ominous sign. She was probably still annoyed with me. I glanced at my watch. It was far too late to call. I'd have to wait until the morning.

Next, I called my voicemail. Jack had left all three messages. It felt both weird and duplicitous to be listening to his voice in Alex's house. Alex had lived there all her life. He must have stood in that bathroom, he'd probably used that toilet and that sink. I wondered if rooms remembered sounds, if they absorbed voices. They do in those ghost-hunting shows on TV; you can buy special equipment which records the ghostly voices captured within the plaster.

The tone of Jack's first message was warm and friendly: 'Hi Lily, it's me. I know you're with Katie tonight but I wanted to ask you about something. Hope you're having a brilliant time. Give me a call when you get a sec.'

In the second message, recorded about an hour later, he sounded irritated: 'Why aren't you answering your phone, Lil? I must have rung about six times. Have you put it on silent? Please call me back.'

The last message made my stomach lurch, horribly: 'I'm worried now,' said Jack, his voice a mixture of anxiety and barely contained anger. 'You've switched your phone off and it's going straight to voicemail. Is everything OK? I'm going to call Katie.'

# Chapter 18
♡

Alex and I both awoke early on Sunday morning, despite having had very little sleep. I think Alex was still high on adrenalin from her party and excited about Ben. I couldn't rest for all the competing thoughts in my head: thoughts about what had happened the night before, about having to deceive Alex and, most pressing of all, about Jack. Why had Jack rung Katie and, more worrying, what had she told him? When could I get away to call her?

I didn't feel comfortable lying (in both senses of the word) in a strange bed, in an unfamiliar bedroom. I looked over at Alex and acknowledged how little I knew her, and how she didn't know me at all, and it made me sad. When you sleep alongside another person it creates a sense of intimacy, and this only served to make me feel more of a fake than ever. Pretending to be someone else is a lonely job, even though you do have two voices competing in your head. I wanted to be at home, in my own bed, where I could be Lily, just plain Lily.

'Laura?' Alex said quietly, when she noticed me stirring. A tiny chink of light was peeking through the curtains and I could just make out her face, her new hairstyle messed up and sticking to her cheeks.

'Uh-huh?'

'I'm sorry about last night.'

'It's OK, it wasn't your fault.'

'Well, I knew you were upset about Jared. I shouldn't have made you play with us.'

'Honestly, it's OK.' Stop being so nice, I thought, I don't deserve it.

'Did you enjoy yourself, apart from that?'

'Yes, it was a great party. Did you?'

She grinned. 'Absolutely. I had a fantastic time. I'm not looking forward to clearing up, though.'

Please don't ask me to stay and help, I thought. I want to get out of here. I need to get out of here. What I said was, 'Well, I can help for a bit,' and hoped for once that she could tell I didn't mean it. 'I promised Mum and Dad I'd come home and do my coursework.'

'Hey, no, you're a guest. I don't expect you to. Jess and a few other people are coming back later to help – it's all arranged.'

'OK, cool. So, what's with you and Ben . . .'

'Me and Ben, what?'

'You know what I mean! So what's the score? Are you seeing each other now?'

'I don't know,' she said, wistfully. 'I guess we'll have to see what happens.'

'But you like him?'

'I think so. Yes.'

'He seems nice. I didn't get to talk to him much, but I think he's cute and I can tell he's into you.'

'Maybe,' she said. 'I'm still not sure if I want a relationship.'

'But it's been well over a year since you and Jack split up.'

She paused. Her brow furrowed and I thought that she gave me a weirdly intense stare, although maybe it was just the way the shaft of light was hitting her face. 'True,' she said, eventually. 'But you know what it's like when you really love someone. It's not that easy to get them out of your head.'

'I don't think Jared and I were as serious as you were,' I said, trying to downplay my imaginary relationship.

'That's trash. I saw how upset you were last night.'

'Nah, it was the punch. And PMT. I get a bit weepy before my period. I'm sorry.'

'Me too, I guess.' She didn't sound convinced. 'So did you find out what he wanted when he called?'

I'd forgotten that she'd been with me when Jack had

rung. 'No. I switched off my phone and then deleted his messages,' I said. 'I don't want to talk to him.'

'You know, you might be better off talking to him and hearing what he has to say,' she said, her voice soft with caution. 'Even if you don't want to get back with him, at least you'll have said everything you want to say, and it will be over properly, with no more ifs and buts. I wish I'd done that with Jack. There was tons of stuff we didn't sort out, you know? He tried to call me for months, but I wouldn't take his calls. I was too upset, and everyone told me I was better off trying to move on with my life. But ever since, I've been wondering how he is and what he's doing, and whether he has any regrets. Sometimes, I wonder whether we could have worked things out, if I'd just let him have his say.'

'Really?' I asked. Facts that for weeks had made no sense to me were now becoming clear. I hadn't understood why Jack had told me that Alex dumped him, when I knew he had initiated the break-up. But it made perfect sense if he'd instantly regretted his decision and wanted Alex back, and she didn't want to know; he'd see that as a final rejection, wouldn't he? In his eyes, she would have been the one who finished the relationship for good.

'Really?' I said again. I swallowed hard. *I* could tell Alex, I thought. I could tell her everything. I could put her out of her misery. I could say, 'It's obvious Jack really loved you because he's as cut up about all this as you are; he can't even bear it when I mention your name. I could say, he's so full of pain and regret that he's convinced himself you finished with him, when I know it's the other way around. And, I hate to admit it, but I still don't think he's completely over you either. Hell, I thought, I could even give you his phone number and his new address. I could invite you both round at the same time and engineer it so you get back together. Maybe that'll be my penance for lying to you both . . .'

'Yeah,' Alex said. 'Ben's great and all, but he isn't Jack. I can't get Jack out of my head. I only wish I could turn back the clock.'

She reached into her bedside drawer and removed something. I couldn't make out what it was, but it sparkled when the light caught it. 'He gave me this,' she said, leaning over to show me. 'I can't wear it, but I haven't had the heart to throw it out.'

It was a gold bracelet, decorated with tiny charms that jangled pleasingly when they knocked against each other. I caught a glimpse of a little dog, a football, a horseshoe and a heart, before Alex took the bracelet back again and replaced it in her drawer. It seemed that she didn't feel comfortable holding it. 'He gave me a charm for each month of our relationship,' she said. 'There are twenty-five altogether. Every month, he'd buy me a new one. Isn't that lovely?'

'Yes,' I agreed. 'It's gorgeous.' Did Jack give all his girlfriends bracelets? Was it his M.O.? I pictured the bracelet Jack had given me and it didn't take a genius to figure out that it wasn't half as special as Alex's. I'm not talking about how much it cost, but of the sentimental value, the thought that had gone into it. There was no contest: he'd liked her more than he would ever like me. I'd always known it, really. It was sad, but there was nothing I could do about it.

'What exactly happened with him, Alex? Please tell me,' I asked. Perhaps it was a brave question, or a stupid one, but it was the reason I was there, after all, and I had a feeling that if she didn't open up now, she never would.

'I don't know . . .' she said, her tone uncertain. 'I haven't really told anyone. Only Jess, and my mum.'

'Don't then.' Did I sound annoyed, rather than concerned? 'I mean, only tell me if it will help.'

'Maybe it will make me feel better about things,' she said. She sighed.

I felt my pulse quicken. Finally, finally, I was going to learn the truth and then all the deceit would have been worth it.

She pulled the duvet tight up to her neck, swaddling herself like a baby. 'There's no point dressing it up. We broke up because he hit me.'

I was so shocked it was almost as if someone had hit me too. I felt winded, unable to breathe or speak. For a moment I even thought I might pass out. I heard a little voice in my head repeating, 'Pull yourself together, Lily, pull yourself together.' How would a normal person react? They'd say something, wouldn't they?

I managed to squeak out: 'Oh my God!'

I don't know what I'd expected Alex to tell me, but it wasn't this. Not in a billion, trillion years. Jack couldn't have hit her; he was gentle, he didn't like violence, he'd tried to protect his mum. Surely she meant Jack's dad had hit her, not Jack? At the same instant I had the thought, I knew that it couldn't have been him – he'd been off the scene years before Jack and Alex met. Maybe I had misheard? What other word sounded like hit? Bit? Spit?

'He hit you? Are you sure?' What a stupid thing to ask. Of course she was sure.

'Yes,' she said. She sat up in bed, still cloaked in the duvet. 'It was horrible.' She was absorbed by her own memories and unaware of my apparent overreaction to her words. I wanted to sob and run out of the room but I knew I had to hold it together. I couldn't allow her to see how upset I was. I wasn't supposed to know Jack; I wasn't supposed to care.

I swallowed hard. 'Had he done it before?' I asked.

'God no. It was a one off.'

That, at least, was a relief. 'So what happened?'

'It was over another guy, a friend of mine called Dom. He wasn't here tonight, we're not friends anymore. Basically, Dom and I got really close at school, just good mates, but Jack didn't like it. There was nothing going on, at least not for me, but I think Dom started to get the wrong idea and one night we got a bit carried away and we ended up kissing. I stopped it and told him it couldn't happen again. It didn't

162

mean anything at all, not to me, anyway. I told Jack because I wanted to be honest. He sort of forgave me, except, after that, he became really jealous and possessive. It wasn't just Dom, it was like he didn't want me to see anyone else, or spend time with anyone else. If he couldn't get hold of me, he'd panic and leave loads of messages. He'd never been like that before . . .'

I shivered, even though I was wrapped snugly in my sleeping bag. Jack hadn't been able to get hold of me last night. Why had he called, anyway? Was it a sign that he was starting to become jealous and possessive of me too? What if he'd found out he couldn't trust me? My urge to leave Alex's house was growing stronger by the minute. It had to find out what Katie had told Jack. Ironic, isn't it, how I'd waited for months for Alex to tell me this story and now that I was finally hearing it, I didn't want to stick around to listen to the details?

Oblivious, Alex continued. 'We started having rows, about stupid things, mainly. And then, one night we ended up arguing about Dom and I got so worked up I told Jack I wished I was with him – Dom – instead because it would be less hassle. He was so incensed he grabbed me by my wrists. He was hurting me and so I tried to push him away and wriggle free. And then he totally lost it and he hit me. It wasn't like he was trying to hurt me, he just lashed out and he caught me on my cheek with the side of his hand, sending me flying. I was so surprised that it didn't even really hurt at first. I was in shock, I think. He tried to see if I was OK but I wouldn't let him come near me. I told him he was just like his father – his dad used to hit his mum, you see – and that he should go home. He was mortified. He kept saying sorry, again and again. He was crying more than me.'

She gasped for air. She'd said all of this in virtually one breath. 'He called me later and apologised again. He asked if he could come round to talk. I hadn't even had time to process what had happened yet, you know? But he'd made up his mind. He said I was right: he was like his dad, and he couldn't be sure he wouldn't do it again. He said I was too good for him and that I deserved better. He told me he loved me, that he'd always love me, but it was over and there was nothing I could say to change his mind. He broke my heart.'

While she was telling me what had happened, I felt I was watching it play out in front of me, like a movie – no, like I was in the room with Jack and Alex. I could see Jack's face and hear his voice, I could even smell his aftershave. I knew the expression he'd be wearing, how he'd be shuffling from foot to foot and chewing his lip. I could see everything except the part where Jack hit Alex; that didn't seem possible.

She was still talking. 'I didn't want anyone to know what had happened; I thought we could sort it out. I had a big bruise so I told everybody that I'd hurt myself playing football – you know, that I was whacked in the face by the ball. Of course, Mum guessed and I couldn't lie to her. She said that if a guy ever hits you, even once, then you should get out straight away. She said however sorry Jack was, however lovely he was most of the time, it didn't matter. Jess said the same thing. So, when Jack started calling again the following week, asking if we could meet up to talk, I said no, he was right, splitting up was for the best. He pleaded with me to give him another chance, to hear him out, at least, but Mum and Jess were telling me not to, and I was so confused, so I said no, even though I really wanted to. He was about to move house again, to another area – he moved around a lot – so it seemed like the right time to end it too, Mum said. I was only sixteen, it was all much too heavy for me. After about a month, Jack stopped calling. He moved away and I haven't heard from him since. I actually tried to ring him once – about six months ago – but I got number not recognised. He must have changed his mobile number.' She sighed. 'Anyway, that's why it's so hard for me to even think about having another relationship.'

I nodded. 'I bet,' I said, my voice barely louder than a whisper. It wasn't much of a response. Again, I asked myself, how would a normal, objective person react to this story, somebody who wasn't overwhelmed, confused and even a little bit frightened by it? I thought of the confessional shows on daytime TV and I tried to pretend that I was the host, and that Alex had just told me her gut-wrenching life story on a show. What would I say? There would be 'oohs' and 'ahs' from the audience, and they would applaud her for being so brave. Then I would turn to her and say something like: 'You've clearly been through a difficult time, but you've come out on the other side, stronger and wiser.'

'It must have been so hard,' is what I finally said. I didn't want to sound like I was reading an autocue. 'Wow. I had no idea.'

It seemed adequate. Alex smiled. 'It's in the past. I don't think about it so much any more.'

Not for me, it isn't, I thought. Jack is my present. I need to get out of here so I can find out what's going on with him.

What I said was: 'Then I think you should give Ben a chance. He could be just what you need.'

'Maybe.'

We both sat in silence for a few minutes, absorbed in our own thoughts. Finally, when I thought it wouldn't be rude to change the subject, I asked, 'What's the time?'

'It's only nine o'clock.'

'Only it's just that I said I'd be home by eleven.'

'Oh right. Let's get up then. What do you fancy for breakfast? Hey, I know there are a few cupcakes left.'

The thought of gooey, sickly sweet icing made me want to throw up. 'I'm not hungry,' I said, climbing out of my sleeping bag without unzipping it. 'Honestly, don't worry about me. Have breakfast after I've gone.'

She appeared disappointed. Was it too obvious that I was trying to get away? 'No worries.'

I pulled on my jeans and shoved my things into my bag,

then went into the bathroom and cleaned my teeth. I looked at my reflection in the bathroom mirror and Laura stared back at me, bleary-eyed and blotchy-faced from too much partying and too little sleep. I combed my hair with my fingers, splashed some water on my face and wiped off the smudged eyeliner with some moistened toilet paper. When I studied myself in the mirror for a second time, I saw an anxious, drained Lily.

Alex's parents were still in bed, so I asked her if she'd tell them goodbye and thanks from me. 'I had a really great time,' I said, when nothing could have been further from the truth. 'Thanks so much again.'

She smiled. 'Call me,' she said, as she gave me a brief hug.

'Course I will. Oh, and happy birthday for tomorrow.'

I shut the front door behind me and took a deep breath. If I'd stayed in that house for one more minute I think I might have spontaneously combusted.

It was only as I walked the short distance to the bus stop that a chilling realisation struck me. I understood why Alex had given me such a strange look earlier that morning when I had brought up her relationship with Jack. Not once, in any of our previous conversations, texts or emails, had she told me her ex's name.

# chapter 19

♡

The bus didn't come for ages. They never do when you're in a hurry. Either that, or they sail straight past you, even though you've got your arm out and a pleading look on your face. I think bus drivers are sadists; they love playing power games, especially with teenagers. If you complain, they say you're lying, or they thought you were going to cause trouble, or you weren't going to pay. Who'd believe you over them? I wondered if I should start walking towards the station, but I had too much to carry and I wasn't sure of the way. And, if I did, a bus was sure to come, right at the point when I was in between stops.

As I stood waiting, I half expected Alex to come running out of her house after me, shouting, 'You're an impostor, Laura Thompson!' Of course, she didn't. She was probably sitting at the kitchen table, eating Cheerios and hoping that her parents hadn't noticed the stains in the carpet. Save for a few cars, the street was quiet, a Sunday morning stillness in the air. I looked around me at the unfamiliar road and the unfamiliar houses and the unfamiliar gardens, and everything appeared skewed, somehow, like it was the wrong size or the wrong colour, or the wrong shape. I felt as if I'd fallen down a hole into another world – like Alice in Wonderland, but without any rabbits or strange people wearing mad hats. Had I made the world look like this, I asked myself, or had it always been this way, and I hadn't noticed?

Someone told me that if a butterfly flaps its wings in one place, it causes a tornado somewhere else. I considered if it might be true. Could I have changed the world for ever? Was it possible that by spending almost a full twenty-four hours as Laura, I had inadvertently made her split off from Lily altogether? Had I changed not just the present, but history too? In some other universe Lily could be waking up in her own bed, as usual, having spent the previous day and evening with Katie or with Jack. A Katie who wasn't annoyed with her. And a sweet, gentle Jack who had never hit anybody in his life, and never would.

The evidence on my mobile phone, still the same as the night before, refuted that. I listened to the messages over and over, trying to find evidence in Jack's voice of the person I now knew he was. There was none. The truth was, nothing had changed at all: it was simply that I knew more than I had before. And how I wished I didn't know. How stupid I was not to have considered that knowing could be worse than not knowing. All the way along, from the moment I'd first tracked down Alex, I'd thought, if I can find out the truth I'll be happy. Knowing was meant to simplify things, not complicate them.

I checked my watch for the umpteenth time. Ten o'clock, still too early to ring Katie. She always lay in on a Sunday. I couldn't risk calling Jack back before I'd spoken to her. He'd have been up for hours, he'd be on his way to football training. What time would he start calling me again? Might he he wait until I rang him? I guessed it depended on what Katie had told him. Oh God, what had she told him?

By the time the bus came and dropped me off at the train station, I couldn't hold back any longer. If Katie were already annoyed with me, waking her up would merely give her something else to be annoyed about. As I dialled her number, I felt a bit sick, the way you do when you're a kid and you know you're about to receive a serious (and deserved) telling off.

'Katie?' I said tentatively.

'For God's sake, Lily! Where the hell have you been? Why didn't you ring me back last night?'

'It's a long story,' I said. 'I'm sorry. I didn't get your message till really late. Is everything OK? Did Jack call you?'

'Yeah, he did.' My pulse quickened. 'That's why I needed to speak to you. He gave me the fright of my life when he called. I didn't even know he had my number.'

'I think I gave it to him once when . . . I can't remember. Sorry. What did he want?'

'He just wanted to speak to you. He didn't say why.'

'Did you tell him I wasn't there?'

'Of course not, Lil. Like I'm going to drop you in it like that? I didn't know what to say, so I told him you had a headache – a migraine – like my mum gets,' she said. 'I said you were asleep and you'd call him this morning. He seemed sort of cool with that. At least, I think he believed me.'

I hadn't been aware that I'd been holding my breath. It came out noisily, like a deflating balloon. Oh, the relief. Katie was a star. Thanks to her, Jack didn't know that I hadn't been at her house all night. No real damage done. I'd never felt so grateful in all my life.

'Thanks, Katie, I owe you one,' I said.

'Yeah, you do. You owe me about a thousand,' she said, and it sounded like she meant to make me pay.

'I know. I appreciate it. Really. If there's anything I can do for you. Anytime.'

She went quiet and I wondered what dreadful tasks she was dreaming up for me. Doing her coursework for a year? Popping the zits on her back?

'There's only one thing,' she said, her tone grave. 'I want you to finish all this Alex stuff. I've had enough of lying for you and pretending I don't mind when you go off to parties and football matches and use me to cover for you. It's not fair.'

'Wow,' I said. I hadn't expected that. 'I'm sorry. I'm really sorry.' I hesitated. This probably wasn't the best time to tell her what I'd learned about Jack. It didn't sound like she'd be sympathetic. But I had to get it off my chest, and preferably before I called him. Katie would know what to do, what to say. 'Listen, Kay,' I continued, cautiously. 'Something's happened and I really need to talk to you. It's about Jack. Can I come round? I'm just getting on the train, but I could be there in an hour or so.'

'No, you can't. Not now, I'm going out with my mum.'

'Please, Katie. It's serious.'

'I can't get out of it,' she said, and it sounded like she was struggling to be firm. 'I promised her. Look, we'll only be out for a few hours. Whatever it is, I'm sure it can wait. Come round later.'

'OK,' I said, flatly. There was no point pushing her.

'What is it about, anyway?'

'It doesn't matter.' This wasn't something I could talk about on the phone, not when she was clearly in a hurry and fed up with the whole Jack situation.

'OK, fine,' she said. I don't think it's unfair to say that she sounded relieved.

Only after I'd put the phone down did I think that I should have asked Katie how long a migraine usually lasts. Hours? Days? Was it feasible that I might still be tucked up in bed, with the curtains pulled tight to block out the light? What I really wanted to know was how much longer I could delay calling Jack back. There was more to it than simply not wanting to talk to him because I didn't know what to say. I couldn't ring him from the train, not with station announcements and train noises and other people talking in the background. Nothing would be more certain to convince him that Katie had lied, and that I had deceived him about where I'd been. '*Sounds like I'm on a train, you say? Yes, it's the latest cure for migraine, didn't you know?*'

But what if he didn't hear from me, couldn't get Katie and so called my house instead? Mum would pick up. She'd learn about my illness and be so concerned that she'd probably drive straight round to Katie's to pick me up. When she arrived, and I wasn't there, the whole charade would disintegrate. I'd be in trouble, Katie would be in trouble, and Jack would be so hurt and angry that . . . that . . . who knew what he might do?

Oh my God, I thought, a cold sensation creeping down my spine. Oh my God, I am actually a little bit scared of him.

I briefly contemplated getting on a train – any train – and seeing where it took me. After all, I was carrying half my wardrobe and all my toiletries with me. I even had my sleeping bag. A quick glance inside my purse revealed I only had fifty-nine pence, barely enough for a bag of crisps. I'm not the park bench type; I wouldn't have lasted an afternoon.

I would have to face Jack, then, but not yet. There was

one thing I could do to buy myself a few more hours before I had to speak to him. I could take the cowardly option: I could text him.

I typed *Srry. Hm bt stl nt wll. Cu l8r. Lxx*

Then, switching off my phone, I climbed on to my train, settled back in my seat and closed my eyes, hoping against hope that I would wake up to find it had all been a bad dream.

# Chapter 20

♡

'Lily, wake up!'

Mum was standing over me, gently shaking my shoulders. I opened my eyes, then promptly shut them again. Why was Mum on the train with me? And since when did train carriages have duvets and pillows? I tried to sit up and speak, but my head felt heavy, my mouth dry and uncooperative.

'Gurr? Wharr? Where am I?'

'You're at home, silly, where you've been for the last three hours. In your own bed. Where did you think you were?'

'I was dreaming I was on a train,' I said, closing my eyes again.

If only it had all been just a dream. Whatever I might have wished for, this wasn't one of those stories where everyone wakes up and lives happily ever after. Real life isn't like that. Not my life, anyhow.

'Ah, that could signify you're going to come into some good fortune,' said Mum, who likes reading books about the meaning of dreams. 'But it probably just signifies that you didn't have enough sleep at Katie's last night. I don't know why you call them sleepovers – you never seem to get any sleep at them. Anyway, you need to get up now. You can't spend all of Sunday in bed, and Jack is downstairs.'

Any hope that Mum's dream analysis was right and I was about to experience good fortune vanished instantly. Panic catapulted the fatigue from my body and I sat up so quickly that I banged my head on the headboard. 'What? Jack? Downstairs?'

'Yes, weren't you expecting him? He arrived a few minutes ago.'

'No,' I said, my voice unexpectedly high-pitched. What could I do to make Mum tell Jack to go home? What could I say? Why couldn't I think of anything? The migraine? Mum would see right through that. I cleared my throat. 'Um, I mean, I'm not sure.'

'Are you OK?' Mum asked, concerned. She gave me her 'you can tell me anything' look and started wittering. 'Have you had a fight? Jack seems to think you're not well. He said something about a migraine, but you didn't mention that when you came home. I didn't know you got migraines. Maybe we need to take you to the doctor on Monday. Are you sure you're all right?'

'Just a headache,' I mumbled. 'It's fine. Nothing to worry about, honest.'

She looked at me sideways, as if she didn't quite believe me. 'Get dressed and come downstairs then. He's in the living room. I'll go and make you both a cup of tea.'

'Thanks,' I said, with a half smile.

She left the room and I looked around me frantically, my eyes scoping out the room like I was in the SAS. Could I climb out of the window and shimmy down the drainpipe to make my escape, like people always seem to do in movies? Or could I could hide under the bed and hope that I'd remain invisible until I chose to climb out again? It worked when I was six, and a fair bit smaller, and before I'd shoved clothes and books and magazines under there, rather than tidy them away. Silly, I know, but Jack wasn't supposed to have come round, unannounced. I'd planned to prepare myself before I saw him again, to think things through properly. I'd expected him to call me, not just to turn up. To call me . . . God, I'd switched off my mobile, hadn't I? Mum said I'd been asleep for three hours. Had Jack been ringing ever since he received my text?

I swung my legs over the side of the bed and walked over to the chair, where I'd dumped my clothes and bags. My phone was buried at the bottom of my handbag. I turned it on and it shuddered into life, announcing, after a brief pause, that I had three missed calls, all from Jack, plus a text from 'Jared' – Alex. I was relieved to see that she had only sent one of those generic, round-robin texts that you send to all your friends at once to save time.

*Thnks 4 cmng. Gr8 2 c u. xxx,* it read. I tossed my phone on the bed. I would reply later, when Jack had gone and when I'd got my head together.

I put my crumpled clothes back on and viewed my reflection in the wardrobe door. If mirrors could speak, mine would have emitted a large and very deep sigh. I looked dreadful: tired, my skin blotchy and my hair a mess of tangles. I'd never usually have let Jack see me looking so ropey, but for once, I didn't care. It's even good, I thought, I really do look like I've had a migraine. Maybe Jack would feel sorry for me and go straight home, so I wouldn't have to face him.

As I came down the stairs I could hear him chatting to Mum in the living room. I couldn't tell what they were saying, but my name was mentioned a couple of times. Sick with nerves, I stood outside the door for a few moments, gathering the courage to push it open. 'Act normal,' I repeated to myself. 'Act normal.' When, finally, I opened the door, Jack jumped up out of his seat and rushed towards me, like a charging bull.

'Lily!' he said, hugging me overenthusiastically. I went through the motions of hugging him back, but I felt I didn't want to get too close. 'Lil,' he continued. 'I've been really worried about you. How's your migraine?'

'S'OK,' I muttered. 'You know.'

Mum gave me a reassuring smile and left the room.

'Come and sit down,' Jack said. He sat back down in his seat and plumped up the cushions for me. 'Look, I'm sorry I dropped in without saying anything first. But I couldn't get hold of you, and then Katie told me you were ill, and then you texted me, and after that you didn't call for hours. I was so worried. I thought you must be really bad.'

'You shouldn't have worried,' I said, avoiding eye contact. 'I turned my phone off, that's all.'

Jack held out his hand to me. I pretended not to notice, shifting in my seat. In my head, a little voice asked, is this the same hand he used to hit Alex? I ignored it. Now that I was with Jack, I wasn't afraid of him, not really. My discomfort had more to do with my growing conviction that he still loved Alex.

When I didn't respond to him, Jack reached over and placed his hand over the top of mine, entwining our fingers together. It didn't feel thrilling, or comforting, like it used to. I knew that if he had the choice, he'd rather be holding her hand.

'Something's wrong,' he said. 'I can tell.'

'No, honest, I'm fine,' I said. I smiled. 'So, er, how was football training?'

'Good. I scored a couple of goals. How was Katie's sleepover?'

'Good,' I said. How lame was this conversation! Jack was usually so easy to talk to. Why couldn't I think of anything to say? Act normal. Act normal.

'Oh right. Cool.' He hesitated. 'Um, Lil, you don't seem yourself.'

'I've had a migraine,' I said. 'You know that. Sorry.'

'Yeah, I know, but it's more than that. It's not just today, it's been a few weeks. Something's up.'

'No, you're imagining it.' I moved my hand away from his, under the pretext that I needed to scratch my nose. Then I remembered seeing a documentary that revealed how touching your nose is a sure sign of lying, and I dropped it to my lap.

'Is it because of what I told you?' he asked.

I shook my head. 'Don't be soft. Of course not.'

No, I thought, it's because of what you *didn't* tell me. Because you only told me half the story. Because it turns out you're not the person I thought you were.

We sat in awkward silence. Mum came in with two steaming mugs of tea and set them down on the coffee table. Jack and I both muttered, 'Thanks,' then went back to staring into our laps. As Mum left the room she gave me a concerned glance.

When she was out of earshot, I asked Jack, 'So why were you trying to call me last night?'

'I needed to ask you something. I've sorted it. It's not important now.'

'Oh,' I said, unsure whether to be relieved or disappointed. All that panic, for nothing.

'I wasn't checking up on you, if that's what you think.'

'No, course not,' I said. Why had he said that? Did it mean he really had been checking up on me? I faked a smile. 'So, everything's cool then.'

'Yeah,' he said, without conviction. He took my hand again and held it to his face. It felt warm and smooth and familiar, and I could feel myself beginning to thaw a little. He drew me towards him and kissed me gently. You can't trust him, said a voice in my head, as I started to respond. I tried to ignore it, but the voice grew louder. You can't trust him. He's not the Jack you thought he was. He hit Alex.

'Not in here,' I said, pulling away. 'My parents are in the kitchen. We should drink our tea.'

'Yeah,' he said, disappointed. He picked up his mug. I noticed it had a picture of Superman on it.

My tea was still too hot and it burned my lips. I carried on sipping it, anyway. We fell back into silence, occasionally peering up at each other, then looking away.

'Why don't we go up to your room?' Jack asked, eventually.

I shook my head.

'Not for *that*. I mean we can talk better there.'

'I don't know . . .' I said. I felt safe in the living room, with my parents on the other side of the wall. And I didn't want to talk to Jack, not now. I wanted him to go home.

'It's not normally a problem, Lil. They know they can trust me, right?'

181

'Sure.' But *I* don't. I don't.

'Come on, then.' He took both of my hands and got up, pulling me with him. 'Mr and Mrs Lawton,' he called out. 'Is it OK if I go up to Lily's room for a few minutes?'

'That's fine!' shouted Mum.

'The door stays open!' shouted Dad.

'Thanks! See,' Jack said to me, grinning, as if he'd won a little victory. 'They're cool with it.'

I didn't know what to say, so I let him lead me up the stairs and into my bedroom. He sat down on the bed and patted the space next to him, beckoning me to join him. As I approached, I noticed that my mobile phone was still lying on top of the duvet where I'd left it, which was now right next to Jack's left leg. He saw it at exactly the same moment.

'Careful, mind your phone,' he said, picking it up. He must have touched a key, rousing it from sleep mode, because, with a beep, it leapt back into life. He glanced downwards and I knew, without looking, that the message from 'Jared' was still displayed on the screen.

The world didn't go into slow motion, like it would have done if this had happened in a film. It skipped a revolution, stopping completely for a second, and then powered back up at double speed up so it could catch up with itself. At least, that's what it felt like.

'Give it here,' I said, trying to snatch the phone from Jack's grasp.

Too late. He'd seen it. He looked at the screen again, as

if he couldn't quite believe what he'd read, and then he looked up at me, with sad, uncomprehending eyes.

'Who's Jared?' he asked. He got up from the bed and stood directly in front of me, holding the phone behind his back.

My heart was pounding so fast, the blood racing so fast to my head, that I needed to sit down, but Jack was blocking my way to the bed.

Who was Jared?

'No one,' I said. Feeble, but in a way, it was the truth. Jared was nobody: just a name I'd snatched out of the air, a name for the imaginary – and now ex-boyfriend of a made-up version of myself. And, for simplicity's sake, 'Jared' was also the moniker I'd given Alex in my phone, to prevent her real name ever flashing up or being viewed in my address book.

Why hadn't I prepared myself for this possibility? All the times I'd feared being caught out, and yet I hadn't considered this one. I'd worried about the consequences of Alex seeing Jack's name on my phone, and I'd worried about what would happen if Jack saw Alex's, but I'd never anticipated that Jack might see the name Jared and question it. What a stupid oversight.

'Don't lie to me, Lily,' Jack said. His tone was flat. 'Who is he?'

Before I could begin to reply, he peered at the phone again and began to read. 'Thanks . . . for . . . coming,' he said, in the slow, deliberate way that people decipher text speak aloud. 'Great . . . to . . . see . . . you.' He paused. 'Kiss. Kiss. Kiss.'

How could Alex's innocent thank-you text to all her party guests suddenly sound so dodgy, so incriminating? The three kisses were just a lazy way of signing off, yet Jack made them seem dirty, nasty, like evidence of cheating. And then it struck me that, technically, I had kissed another guy. I hadn't wanted to, but I'd done it.

'Who is he?' he repeated. 'What were you doing with him last night, when you said you were at Katie's? Where were you?'

'It's not what you think,' I said. I felt so light-headed and panicky that I couldn't process my thoughts. 'You've got it all wrong . . .'

'You said you had a migraine. I even felt sorry for you. I was worried about you.'

'I'm sorry,' I said, unsure what I was apologising for. I didn't know which words to use next. I had the impression that whatever I came up with, Jack wouldn't believe me. What exactly could I say? Not the truth, certainly: *'Jared isn't a guy, he's a girl. And, he isn't just any girl, he's really your ex-girlfriend Alex, whom I've been meeting in secret. Oh, and by the way, Alex thinks I'm called Laura. And Laura had a pretend boyfriend called Jared too.'*

My real-life story sounded so preposterous that even Jerry Springer wouldn't contemplate having me on his show to explain it. Then again, maybe it was so ridiculous that nobody could even have made it up, which meant that Jack would have to believe me. Was this the time to confess everything? How might he react? And what was worse: allowing him to think I'd spent last night with a guy called Jared and that I'd lied about it, or telling him I'd been deceiving him for months by spending time with his ex-girlfriend?

It came down to this: which would make him more upset? What might make him angrier? Which might make him lose control altogether, like he had with Alex?

'You've got to believe me,' I said, pleading. 'I'm not seeing another guy. Jared is just someone who was there last night. That text was sent to everyone, not just me.'

It wasn't exactly the truth, but it wasn't a lie, either.

'I don't believe you,' he said. 'I want to, but I can't. Katie was in on it too, wasn't she? She lied for you. How many other times has she done that?'

I looked up at him and saw how much pain there was in his eyes, how red his cheeks had grown, and I felt myself begin to tremble. Was this what he looked like when he was about to lash out?

'You've been acting off for weeks and weeks,' he said. 'I know there's something going on. I tell you what, if it's all so innocent, why don't we call Jared back now?'

'No!' I cried. My voice came out far louder, far higher pitched than I'd expected. It was such a strong, instinctive reaction that Jack read it as a sure sign of my guilt. Holding the phone above his head, far out of my reach, he began to attempt to ring 'Jared'.

'No!' I cried again. The thought of what might happen if Alex answered the phone to Jack terrified me so much that I'd have done anything to prevent it. I clambered up on to the bed and began grasping for the phone, making it impossible for Jack to dial. Eventually, he gave up trying and gripped me by my wrists, in exactly the way Alex had described. Panicking, I tried to grapple free. I was near the edge of the bed, finding it hard to balance, to right myself.

'Calm down, Lily,' Jack said, grasping me tighter. 'Stop it.'

'Let go!'

'Not until you calm down,' he said. His jaw was clenched tight, his eyes steely.

'You're hurting me!'

I put all my strength into one last violent, twisting pull, succeeding in freeing my arms from his grip. But the shock of being released, combined with the unexpected pain of the friction burns from Jack's hands, sent me careering off balance. As he let go, I fell sideways from the bed, my arms and legs flailing pointlessly. In the moment before I hit the floor, the corner of the bedside table came up to meet me. There was sound like snapping wood and I felt a sharp pain in the side of my head.

I lay, dazed, for what felt like minutes, but was probably only a few seconds. My head hurt. I touched it with my fingers and felt wetness. Warm, sticky wetness.

'Oh my God, Lil, are you OK?' I looked up to see Jack crouching over me. There was no colour in his face. 'I tried to stop you falling but you were too quick.'

'Leave me alone,' I said, instinctively drawing my knees to my chest. He flinched.

'Oh God, you're bleeding. Don't move, I'll get help.'

'Go away,' I whimpered. 'Don't touch me.'

He backed away from me, an expression of utter bewilderment in his eyes. 'I'm sorry, I'm sorry,' he repeated. 'I'd never hurt you. It was an accident. I'll go and get help.'

He ran into the hall. Simultaneously, I heard my parents rushing up the stairs.

'We heard a crash,' said Dad. 'What's happened?'

'There's been an accident,' Jack said. 'It was an accident. Lily fell off the bed. She's cut her head.'

Mum and Dad pushed past him into the room. 'Are you OK, Lily?' Mum asked. I'd managed to drag myself up into a sitting position, but the sensation of blood pumping from my head was making me feel sick and weak.

'I don't know,' I said. 'I feel a bit strange.'

'Did you lose consciousness at all?'

'I'm not sure. I can't remember. I don't think so.'

Dad leaned over me. 'It's just a little cut,' he said. 'Head wounds always bleed a lot. I'm sure it looks a lot worse than it is. But I think we should get you checked over in case you're concussed.'

I began to sob. Knowing you have to go to hospital always makes an accident seem more serious, and the shock was wearing off now. Dad stroked my back, while Mum went to find some antiseptic and a bandage.

Jack hovered by the door. 'Is she OK?' he asked, meekly.

'She'll be fine,' said Dad. 'Don't worry. You can come in if you like.'

Jack hesitated. He took a step into the room and tried to make eye contact with me, but I couldn't meet his gaze. He stepped back again. 'I think I should go,' he said. 'I'm just in the way. Tell Lily I hope she's OK and that I'm sorry.'

'You can tell her yourself,' said Dad, puzzled. 'She's right here. Come with us to Casualty if you like.'

But Jack was already halfway down the stairs. A second later, we heard the front door slam behind him, and he was gone.

# Chapter 21

♡

The irony isn't lost on me, but in the hours following my accident I gradually developed the worst headache I've ever experienced. I have no way of knowing if it was as bad as the migraine I'd pretended to have the night before, as I've never had a real migraine, but it was a piercing, pounding pain which drummed into my skull every time I moved my head. While I couldn't admit it to my parents, I was fairly certain that the headache was caused as much by my anxiety about Jack as by my unfortunate dive on to my bedside table.

We didn't have to spend too long at the hospital. It turns out that head injury patients are A-list celebrities in the world of sickness and accidents so, rather than sit on the hard plastic chairs in the waiting room for hours on end, like we did when I sprained my ankle, we were shown straight through to a cubicle. The doctor examined me and made me do a series of weird exercises, all of which must have been designed to make me look stupid, like smiling fakely at him, and asking me to follow his pencil with my eyes. Then he asked me questions about how I felt, such as, was I feeling very tired or confused, and did I feel nauseous? Even though I did feel like throwing up, and I was absolutely done in, I answered no to everything, for fear I'd have to stay there overnight.

I remember thinking it was funny how the signs of concussion were almost identical to the symptoms of 'Jack-itis' – the very same feelings I'd been experiencing since Alex had told me what he'd done. How could I tell whether I felt sick and dizzy because my head was about to fall off, or to explode (or whatever it is that happens when you're concussed), or because I was upset and confused about Jack?

'If she does start to feel disoriented, or nauseous, or drowsy, bring her straight back in,' the doctor said to my parents, before discharging me. I didn't even need stitches. He recommended that I should take a couple of days off school to rest, which really pleased me, not least because my hair was matted with dried blood and I wasn't allowed to wash it for a few days, until my wound had started to heal.

I expected to arrive home from the hospital to find at least one message from Jack, but he hadn't called at all. When I tried several times to ring to him to let him know I was OK, his phone went straight to voicemail. I left a short message saying I was all right and I hoped he was too. But by the time I went to sleep – or tried to – he still hadn't called back. Not knowing what he was thinking or why he wouldn't get in touch was unbearable. I couldn't figure out if he was angry with me, or scared. Surely it couldn't be that he just didn't care? Was he avoiding me because he still believed I was cheating on him with a guy named Jared, or because he thought I blamed him for my fall? And did I blame him? Even I couldn't say for sure. Jack hadn't pushed me, that was clear, but if he hadn't frightened me so much by becoming angry and grabbing hold of my wrists, then I wouldn't have fallen, would I? Or was it my fault for climbing on the bed? Or my fault for lying to Jack? Or his, for what he did to Alex? Everything was such a blur. I couldn't make sense of any of it.

Concerned, my parents kept asking me what was going on between us. Dad said Jack had acted so strangely after my accident that something must have happened. I denied everything. 'We're fine,' I said. 'Jack is just squeamish about blood, that's all.' I didn't tell them Jack hadn't even rung to find out how I was.

Katie came round later in the evening to cheer me up. She said she couldn't stay annoyed with me any longer, not when I was so desperate to speak to her that I'd thrown myself off my bed just to get her attention. Joking aside, I think she might have felt guilty; if she'd let me come round when I'd asked, the accident wouldn't have happened.

'God, you look a state,' she told me, when she arrived to find me in bed, propped up on a pile of cushions. 'Mind you, you've always said you wanted to try red highlights.'

'Yeah,' I said, dryly. 'Boots was out of henna.'

She hugged me tightly and I had a proper cry for the first time all day, letting all my fear and sadness and confusion and exhaustion pour out in a stream of tears and snot. When I'd calmed down and wiped my eyes and blown my nose, I filled Katie in on everything that had happened over the past twenty-four hours. I described to her the party, the game of spin the bottle, Alex's revelation about Jack, and his reaction to the message from 'Jared' on my phone. It was hard to believe it had all taken place in just one day. She let me go on and on, uninterrupted, until I'd finished. I must have talked for almost an hour. I felt better afterwards, my head easier, my thoughts less tangled.

'Wow, it's all such a mess,' she said.

'I know,' I whimpered. 'I really hate myself. I've ruined everything.'

'No, you haven't,' she said, but I knew she was just being kind. 'It'll be alright, I promise.'

'How?' I asked.

'I don't know yet, but it will.' She paused. 'I just can't get over Jack hitting Alex. I don't know him like you do, obviously, but it doesn't sound like him. Especially after what he said about his dad and all.'

'I don't think he meant to hurt her,' I said. I remembered the horrible sensation of his hands pressing down on my wrists. 'I don't think he knows how strong he is.'

'So maybe it's genetic,' suggested Katie. 'Maybe he

couldn't help himself.'

That explanation hadn't occurred to me. I didn't like it. 'Don't say that. He's not a bad person. I've known him for months and months and he's never hit anyone. He hates fighting. If anyone starts on him, he walks away.'

'Well, then, maybe he's changed. Just because he hit Alex once doesn't mean he'd do it again. We've all done stuff we regret in the past.'

'You're right,' I said. 'Oh God, Kay. What am I going to do? He won't answer his phone, so I can't even try to sort it out, even if I knew what I wanted to say.'

She put her hand on my shoulder, firmly. 'There's only one thing you can say. I know I've been banging on about this for ages, but I think you've got to come clean with him. You've got to tell him the truth, all of it.'

'I can't,' I said. 'He'll hate me. He'll never talk to me again.'

'You don't know that.'

'Yeah, I do. He won't understand. Who would? And then I'll lose him. And the only reason I started all this was because I liked him and wanted to get closer to him . . .'

'That, and because tracking down and befriending Alex was a bit of a thrill, admit it. I was there, remember? It was a laugh.'

'Only at first. Then I got to know her. She's really nice, you'd like her if you met her.'

'That's not going to happen,' said Katie. 'I know you don't want to hurt her, but you've got to tell her the truth

193

too. Whatever happens with Jack, you can't keep on dressing up and calling yourself Laura Thompson every couple of weeks. Look how stressful it's been.'

I nodded, and sniffed. 'I know. She'll really hate me, won't she?'

'I don't know. She might see the funny side. Eventually.'

'Stop trying to make me feel better. She'll probably try to get me arrested, or put a hit out on me. I deserve it.' I laughed, flatly. 'It might be simpler just to ask my parents if I can legally change my name to Laura Thompson.'

'Yeah, and while you're at it I'll get mine changed to Kylie Minogue. But it won't make me a forty-something, blonde Australian pop princess.'

'Fair point.' Katie can always be relied upon to tell it how it is.

'Terminate Project Jared, it is then,' she said. 'Finally. I guess it took a knock on the head to make you come to your senses. Promise you'll do it? I promise I'll be here for you.'

'I promise,' I said. 'I'm home all day tomorrow. I'm going to lie here and work out exactly what to say to both of them.' I smiled, even though I felt like I was on death row.

'It'll be fine,' she said. Smirking, she raised her left eyebrow. 'But if it isn't, and you have to flee the country, can I have your new iPod and your red patent Mary-Janes?'

# Chapter 22

♡

When I think about it, there are a million and one reasons why I did it.

I did it because Jack was perfect and I knew there must be more to him.

I did it because I wanted to understand him better and I thought that finding out about his past would help me feel closer to him.

I did it because I was curious about his relationship with Alex.

I did it because I was bored.

I did it because I wanted to, and because I couldn't help myself.

I did it because once I'd started, I didn't know how to stop.

But, most of all, I did it because I could.

A million and one reasons, but still the same result.

* * *

I finally heard from Jack on Monday evening. Maybe he didn't realise I was off school, or maybe it took him until then to get his head together. I don't know; I didn't ask. He rang to say he wanted to talk and asked if he could come round after dinner. He sounded weird, flat, like he hadn't slept all night. I probably sounded that way too.

I tried to make myself look vaguely attractive, which is quite difficult when your hair is greasy and has dried blood stuck in it, and you've had no sleep. I honestly don't know why I cared what I looked like; he was going to hate me anyway, when I told him what I'd done. I guess I'd rather be disliked than thought ugly. Does that make me shallow?

Although I'd spent all day planning what I was going to say to him, when he arrived I found myself fumbling for words. I didn't know if I should kiss him hello, or touch him at all. We were so awkward with each other that if a stranger had observed us, they'd have thought we had just met. We went into the living room and sat on the sofa, with a good few inches' space between us. Neither of us suggested going to my bedroom, to revisit the scene of my accident.

Jack spoke first. 'I'm sorry,' he said, quietly. 'I didn't mean to run out on you yesterday. I was freaked out by what happened. Your parents were there, and then I saw you were OK, and I thought you'd be better off with them.'

'It's all right,' I said. It struck me that I wasn't at all scared of him any more. I just felt sad.

'I didn't mean to hurt you. You know that, right?'

I nodded. 'Course not.'

'It all got out of hand. I was trying to stop you, to make you calm down. That's why I got hold of your wrists – it was a self-defence move, a wrist lock – but you were thrashing around so much I think I did it wrong.'

'Oh,' I said. 'I didn't know that.'

'I must have let go just as you pulled away from me. I tried to catch you but you fell too fast.'

He held out his hand to me, like a peace offering. I took it, slipping his fingers between mine and he smiled, a half smile. For a moment, I could almost let myself believe everything would be fine.

'It's all right,' I said, softly.

'No, it's not.' He withdrew his hand and took a deep breath. 'You thought I was going to hit you. Didn't you?'

'No,' I said, unconvincingly. 'I was confused and upset. I just panicked.'

He shook his head. 'I know it, I could see it: you were scared of me. I've seen that look before, the fear in your eyes. Maybe you weren't even conscious of it, but the look you gave me when you were on the bed, just before you fell, that's the exact expression my mum used to get on her face when my dad was about to hit her. I've seen it too many times not to recognise it.'

I didn't say anything. What was the use in denying it? He'd convinced himself it was true, and what's more, he was right. When, in just a few minutes, I told him what I knew about Alex, he'd understand why, too.

'I guess I'm just like my dad, after all,' he said, his body appearing to crumple up, as if it was weighed down with regret and shame. 'I've tried so hard not to be, but it hasn't worked. I keep going over and over it in my mind and I still can't say for certain that I wouldn't have lost it last night, if you hadn't fallen. I was so angry and jealous and wound up, just like he used to get.'

'That's rubbish. You're not like him.'

'But I am,' he said. 'I've done it before.' His voice was so quiet that it was almost as if he hoped I wouldn't hear. 'I hit a girl once.'

I swallowed hard. Time to confess. I couldn't let him go on thinking he was the bad guy. 'I know,' I said. My voice came out in a barely audible squeak, as if it didn't want to relay the information I was making it say. I cleared my throat. 'I know what happened with Alex. I know everything.'

All those months of keeping my secret from him – torturing myself, making up lies and stories and excuses – and in only a moment, with just a few simple words, in one short breath, it was out.

Jack looked at me, startled, confused. 'What do you mean?'

I couldn't make eye contact. I looked slightly to the left of him, at a little speck of dust on the wall. 'She told me herself,' I said to the speck. 'It was her text message you saw last night, not another guy's. I've been in contact with her for months. It's a long story . . .'

I didn't tell Jack everything, just the bits I felt he needed to know and which wouldn't hurt him unnecessarily. He didn't need to be told that his treasured Arsenal scarf wasn't meant as a gift, or that I'd celebrated Alex's eighteenth birthday with her. I wasn't trying to make myself look better; guys tend to prefer to hear the edited highlights, rather than an in-depth account with every word and every feeling described. If anything, I came out of it all looking worse. I said sorry a lot, and 'I shouldn't have done that,' and 'I didn't mean to hurt you,' but they're just words. They don't change anything, or make things better.

'You're unbelievable,' said Jack. He'd said a lot of other things while I was talking, most of them unintelligible, or unrepeatable. He stared at me – through me – like I was Gollum, disgusting and withered and covered in slime. 'I don't know you at all, do I?' he stated. 'I wasn't paranoid. I was right that you were acting odd, and right not to trust you.'

'And I was right that you were hiding stuff.'

'I might have told you, one day. I told you about my dad, didn't I?' He thought for a second. 'Then again, I might not ever have told you what happened with Alex. It wasn't your business. You can know someone well without knowing every single thing they've ever said and done. I think I knew it would change things, make you think of me differently. I was right, wasn't I?'

'I guess so.'

'So does Alex know now? Does she know who you are, and about us?'

I shook my head. 'I haven't told her yet. I wanted to tell you first.'

'Uh huh.' He seemed lost in thought. Was he wondering about Alex, picturing her, missing her? 'She needs to know. It's not fair to keep on lying to her.'

'I know,' I said. 'I'm going to tell her, as soon as I've worked out what to say. But listen, there's something else you need to know. It's not to do with Alex. I looked up your dad. On the web. I wanted to tell you at the time but I didn't know how to.'

'You had no right.'

'I know, I'm sorry,' I said. 'I Googled him, that's all. I swear. I didn't do any more than that.'

'How did you know his name? I didn't tell you it.'

'I worked it out. You told me his surname, and the rest I just pieced together.'

'Jesus, Lily, you should get a job on the *Sun*, or become a private detective or something. Pretending to be someone else, tracking down my dad . . . I had no idea how sneaky you could be. Then again, I guess I didn't know you at all.'

That stung, more than it should have done.

'I was curious. I wanted to understand you better. I

couldn't imagine what he was like, what he looked like, so I had to find out for myself.'

'Yeah, whatever. So tell me about my father. Is he still a teacher, then? Is he still fooling people that he's a great guy?'

'Do you really want to know? I won't tell you stuff if you'd rather not hear it.'

'Oh, no, please do,' he said, sarcastically. 'Although, I suppose if you don't I can just Google him, can't I?'

I ignored his dig. 'All right, then. He's a headteacher now.'

'That figures. Still charming his way up the ladder. What else?'

'Not much,' I said. 'He lives in Luton. There was also something about a chemistry prize. And,' I hesitated. 'And, he got married again.'

'Really?' said Jack. 'Mum'll be pleased. So he's got a new punchbag, then. Maybe that's why he's left us alone for a while. So what else did your investigation uncover?'

Should I tell Jack about his little brother or sister? If he didn't know his dad had married again, it would come as another shock. But I had to, didn't I?

'I don't want to upset you,' I said, hesitant. 'More than I already have, I mean.'

'Go on, hit me with it.' He laughed. 'Sorry. That was bad taste. What is it?'

'OK. He has another kid, a young child, the website said. That's all I know, I swear.'

'Poor sucker,' he said. 'Boy or girl?'

'I don't know. It didn't say.'

'So I've got a half-brother or sister somewhere out there and it was on the internet, and I didn't know. That's pretty mind-blowing.'

I nodded. 'Are you glad I told you?'

'I dunno,' he said. 'I have absolutely no idea how I feel about anything right now.'

'Even me?' I ventured.

'Especially you.'

At least he hadn't said he hated me. I gazed at the floor. I felt empty, like my insides had shrivelled up. 'So what are you going to do?' I asked.

'I haven't got a clue. I've just found out that pretty much everything in our relationship has been a lie, from start to finish, and that I've got family I didn't know existed. What would you do?'

'It hasn't all been a lie,' I said. 'I never told you anything that wasn't true, I just left a lot out. God, I know that sounds lame. What I'm trying to say is I really do like you. I didn't lie about that.'

'Yeah? I really liked you too.' He emphasised the 'd', making it clear his feelings were past tense, that it was over. 'I thought me and you could have been perfect together. But it turns out that you didn't trust me and I *can't* trust you, so where does that leave us?'

I shrugged my shoulders. 'I don't know . . .' I knew it

was hopeless, but a little part of me was still wishing he might say we could work things out and start again.

'Exactly. Nowhere.'

'I'm sorry,' I said. 'I really am.'

He smiled. 'Me too.' He got up from the sofa. 'I think I should go home now. I need to sort my head out – I've got a lot to think about. And you need to rest.'

'OK.' My eyes stung with embryonic tears. I sat forward, readying myself to get up and see him out, but he shook his head and waved me down again. I was glad. It meant there'd be no awkward goodbye at the front door.

'Take care of yourself, Lily,' he said. 'It's been . . . interesting.'

As he walked past me into the hall, I held my breath to stop the tears from coming, and thought, when he tells people about his last girlfriend, how's he going to say it ended?

And, with a click of the latch, what started on a damp stone wall, a little over six months ago, was done for good.

# Chapter 23
♡

*Topfriendz*
*Inbox: 1 message*
*From: Alex*
*Subject: *!*!*!*
*Lily,*
*I know everything.*
*Please don't try to contact me.*
*Goodbye,*
*Alex*

That's what I woke up to this morning, my eyes still puffy from crying about Jack. Laura had been unmasked, like the villain in a kid's cartoon. It should have come as a massive shock, but it didn't. Perhaps, after all the drama of the past few days, I am already so numb that nothing else can touch me. Maybe I was concussed, after all. Or maybe, I half expected it. Jack hadn't said he was going to tell Alex, but that was the only possible explanation. I don't think it was about revenge, but because he thought she should know, and he didn't trust me to tell her. I can't really blame him for that, with my track record. I didn't – and don't – feel angry about it. In a way, it made things easier for me. It meant I didn't have to spring the truth on Alex myself, to find the words to say the unsayable.

The hardest thing was not being able to do anything about the message for hours. I couldn't even speak to Katie because she was in school, with her mobile switched off. So I left it up on the screen all morning, reading it over and over and trying to imagine what Alex must have felt when Jack suddenly called her, out of the blue, after all this time. And then I wondered what she'd thought when he'd told her about me, how her pleasure and surprise at hearing from him must, in a flash, have turned to dismay and anger. It hurt to think of the two of them talking, doubtless bonding again over what a bitch I was, and how stupid they'd been to like me. Maybe they are back together already, everything forgiven and forgotten, with the whole Lily/Laura saga consigned to history, just an anecdote, a tiny blip in their lives. Is this all I'll be to Jack? A mistake? A bad memory?

Katie called at lunchtime, which was a very good thing, as it stopped me feeling quite so sorry for myself. She had the reaction I should have had when I saw Alex's message: horror and disbelief.

'Are you sure it was Jack who told her?' she asked, when she'd stopped screeching 'Oh my God!' at me.

'No one else knows,' I said. 'Except you, of course. And, if you'd told her, that really would be twisted.'

'Yeah, right, as if. So, are you going to reply to her? I know she says not to, but I think you should. You need to find out what she's going to do.'

'What's the point? She won't believe a word I say.'

'You'll feel better,' said Katie. 'Otherwise you'll just keep going over and over it in your head.'

I decided Katie was right and, before I could chicken out, quickly left Alex a voicemail: 'Hi, it's, er, Lily,' I began. It was weird saying my real name when she'd only ever known me as Laura. 'I guess Jack told you. I'm really sorry about everything. I know you don't want to talk to me, but it would mean a lot to me if you'd just give me the chance to explain and say sorry properly. I promise I won't call you again.'

She made me sweat for six whole hours. Thirty minutes ago, her number flashed up *Jared*; there hadn't seemed much point changing it to *Alex* in my address book.

'OK, then, I want to hear what you've got to say,' she said, coldly, without any introduction. I got the impression that she'd had to steel herself to do it, and it sounded like there was someone else in the room with her. Her mum?

Jessica? I hadn't thought: there'd be a whole line of people queuing up to hate me now, wouldn't there?

'I'm sorry,' I said. How many times have I used that word over the past few days? 'I never meant to lie to you or to upset you.'

'Is that it?' she said. 'You're sorry? Have you any idea what you've done? Who the hell do you think you are, Lily, if that's even your real name? Are you some kind of psychopath?' She was speaking so fast it was as if she was frightened to keep the words in her mouth. 'You stayed at my house, you came to football with me, I introduced you to my friends. You spent time with my parents . . . Oh my God, what am I going to tell them? They liked you. Shit, I even felt sorry for you over Jared, *a guy who never even existed*. Do you think I'm a mug? Did you laugh about me with your mates? Did you?'

She stopped, because she'd run out of breath. I'm sure she had plenty more to say.

'God, no,' I said. 'It wasn't like that at all. It was a laugh for all of five minutes, if that. I started it because I wanted to find out about Jack, that's all.'

'So you used me?'

I nodded, my eyes downcast with shame, even though she couldn't see me. 'I'm so sorry. I didn't think of you as a person at first, just a name and a picture on Topfriendz. Once I met you it was different. I know it sounds crazy but I was starting to think of you as a proper friend. I wanted to tell you the truth, loads of times, but I didn't know how.'

'How about, "Hello Alex, my name's not Laura, it's Lily, and I'm a pathological liar,"?'

That stumped me.

'You know, I could report you, get you banned from Topfriendz. I could probably even tell the police about you, if I wanted.'

'I know,' I said.

'I'm not going to, though. I'd rather just pretend you never existed. Do you know the worst thing? I had doubts about you all the way along, but I ignored them. The really basic stuff you didn't know about football, the fact you didn't seem to do anything on Topfriendz except talk to me occasionally, and that all your friends were random people . . . Sometimes you contradicted yourself too, or brought up stuff you couldn't have known about. And when I think about it, you asked way too many questions about Jack. But I explained everything away. I liked you because you were easy to talk to, because you made me laugh. I thought you were ditzy, a bit flaky, maybe a bit immature too. But then, of course, you are only fifteen. Jess even said she had a bad feeling about you, and I defended you. I thought she didn't like you because she was jealous.

'Last night, after Jack called, I got out my old photo albums from when I was a kid, and found some pictures from the sports camps I went to. There was nobody in any of the photos who looked liked you. There was a girl called Laura, but she had a much darker complexion and completely different features. I should have checked sooner. Maybe it's my fault. I shouldn't have been so trusting. I didn't realise there were people out there who got a kick out of pretending to be someone else.'

Is that how she saw me? Some sort of pervert? 'I'm not like that,' I said. 'I know I'm a liar, but I'm not a freak.'

'Actually, you're a pretty bad liar,' she said. 'And a terrible actor.'

'I know. But I'm not a bad person, honestly.'

'I don't really care. You did a bad thing, and that's what counts. But you know that. And you're paying for it big time. I know for a fact that Jack doesn't want anything more to do with you.'

I winced. It was horrible hearing that from Alex, knowing she and Jack had discussed my shortcomings. I thought, she must have loved saying it, even if she didn't let it show.

'I feel sorry for you,' she said. 'You messed up what could have really good for you. But do you know the funniest thing? In a strange way I'm actually kind of glad all this happened. It's made Jack get back in touch with me, which he probably wouldn't have done otherwise. It's got us talking again. So I suppose I should be thanking you.'

'Do you think you're going to get back together?' I didn't want her to say yes, even though I knew there was no hope for Jack and me.

'I doubt it,' she said. 'Who knows? To be honest, I don't think I'd tell you even if I did.'

'I think he still loves you,' I said. 'For what it's worth, I think he always has. I'm not making excuses for what I did, but that was part of it. I couldn't compete.'

'Oh,' she exclaimed, taken aback. She composed herself. 'It's big of you to tell me that.' She paused again. 'You know, I think that maybe we could have been friends – real friends – if we'd met some other way, and there wasn't a Jack. In another life, maybe.'

'Me too.'

There was a silence. The gaps between our sentences were growing larger, and I knew the conversation was coming to its conclusion.

'Please will you tell your parents I'm sorry,' I said. 'I'll send your dad the money for the ticket and the scarf.'

'No, please don't. I'm not going to tell them what's happened. They'd be too hurt, and they already worry about me talking to people on Topfriendz. I don't want to confirm their fears. I think I'll just tell them we had a big fight and aren't friends any more. I'll just make something up.'

'OK,' I said. I don't know why it mattered, but I hoped she wouldn't say anything too horrible.

'Can I just check something?' She laughed, nervously. 'You're not a Tottenham fan, are you? Because that I really couldn't forgive.'

'No, Alex. I'm a Gooner through and through. If I were ever genuinely to support a football team, it would be Arsenal.'

'That's OK, then.'

There was another silence. I felt so drained, so empty, that even the annoying voice in my head, the one that never shuts up, couldn't think of anything to say.

Alex took a deep breath. 'All right, I'm going to hang up now. I meant what I said before. After I've put the phone down, please don't call me or text me or message me.'

'I won't. I promise. I'm going to delete Laura's profile right now. You'll never hear or see from me again.'

'Good,' she said. 'I mean that in the nicest possible way.'

I laughed, a hollow laugh. 'Bye, Alex.'

'Bye, Lily,' she said. 'Oh, and goodbye, Laura.'

# Chapter 24

♡

*RIP Laura Thompson*
*January 2009 - April 2009*
*She will be dearly missed by all her friends*
*on Topfriendz, especially by Igor*
*and by her alter ego, Lily Lawton*

Laura Thompson doesn't exist any more. A few minutes ago, I deleted her profile from Topfriendz. Murder in cyberspace is quick and bloodless; I don't think Laura felt a thing.

I'm not certain that she's really gone, though. I read somewhere that you can never fully delete something that's been on the web. There are always traces of it, ghost pages, hiding somewhere. One day, if they wanted to, someone with more technical know-how than me could resurrect

Laura. And I'm sure that if they compared her profile to the others on Topfriendz, they wouldn't be able to tell that she wasn't a real person. There are probably thousands of Lauras out there: made-up people who vanish into the ether like grains of cyber sand, the moment you switch off your broadband connection.

She'll always be part of me, of course: there whenever I think of Jack, or Alex. If it weren't for Laura, I wouldn't know about football, or how to make great cupcakes, or how to get the train to the other side of London on my own. Living with her for six months has changed me. I feel ten years older and about a hundred years wiser.

I've always thought there must be a reason why the word 'dual' is in 'individual'. Now I think I know why. Maybe we all have a Laura inside us, a person we could have been, a somebody who says and does the things we wouldn't dare to do, who asks what we dare not ask.

I do know there's no point searching for the 'perfect' boyfriend, not unless you really do want to date a Ken doll. Everyone has bruises and blemishes, and some of them are hidden on the inside, so deep that even you and I don't know they're there. If you look too hard for them, if you push and push, you'll only end up creating new ones.

It's always good to have questions, but sometimes, it's better not to ask.

Also available by Hilary Freeman

Naomi is restless. She's on her gap year and stuck at home with her parents while all her friends are travelling or away at university. Then she meets Danny, a mysterious and intense musician who opens her eyes to a whole new world around her. Danny is exciting and talented, and his band are on the brink of stardom. But he also has a dark, destructive side . . .

Will Naomi be able to save Danny before it's too late? And, more importantly, can she save herself?

'Warm, witty, compelling and insightful, it's a great read.'
*Sunday Express*

☆

# www.piccadillypress.co.uk

☆ The latest news on forthcoming books

☆ Chapter previews

☆ Author biographies

☆ Fun quizzes

☆ Reader reviews

☆ Competitions and fab prizes

☆ Book features and cool downloads

☆ And much, much more . . .

## Log on and check it out!

*Piccadilly Press*